THE **DEVASTATORS**

DONALD HAMILTON

A **MATT HELM** NOVEL

THE **DEVASTATORS**

TITAN BOOKS

The Devastators
Print edition ISBN: 9781783292882
E-book edition ISBN: 9781783292899

Published by Titan Books
A division of Titan Publishing Group Ltd
144 Southwark Street, London SE1 0UP

First edition: April 2014
1 2 3 4 5 6 7 8 9 10

Did you enjoy this book? We love to hear from our readers.
Please email us at readerfeedback@titanemail.com or write to us at
Reader Feedback at the above address.

To receive advance information, news, competitions, and exclusive
offers online, please sign up for the Titan newsletter on our website:
www.titanbooks.com

THE **DEVASTATORS**

1

I made my bride's acquaintance at Kennedy Airport,
formerly Idlewild, just in time for us to commence our
honeymoon by catching the ten p.m. jet to London. It
wasn't the first time I'd acquired a wife in the line of duty,
but it was the first time I'd done it sight unseen.

I'd been informed that the girl's code name was Claire,
and that she was small—five-two, one-oh-five—and
blonde and tanned and competent. It had been explained
to me that they were hauling her back from the Far East
somewhere to do this job with me, and that she was
coming straight through, briefed and costumed and
inoculated on the way, so there would be no opportunity
for advance introductions.

"We needed a female agent who had never operated
in Europe," Mac had told me in his Washington office
on the second floor of an obscure building in an obscure
street, never mind the name. "I do not think she will be
recognized there. I hope not."

"I've operated in Europe, sir," I said.

He looked at me across the desk. It was hard to read his expression for the sunlit window behind him—not that his expression is ever easy to read, whatever the direction of the light. I'd known him a long time, and if his hair was gray, it was no grayer now than when I'd first met him. His eyebrows were still startlingly black. Maybe he dyed them for effect. It was, I knew, a matter for speculation among the younger members of the outfit. As far as I was concerned, his eyebrows were his own business. I wasn't about to ask. I'll buck him on something important, but not on eyebrows.

"*You* are supposed to be recognized, Eric," he said, using my code name for emphasis.

"I see," I said, although that was a slight exaggeration.

"You are the stalking-horse," he said. "You will travel under your own name, openly. You are Matthew Helm, a U.S. undercover agent—but ostensibly you are off duty for the moment. You have just married a lovely young girl after a whirlwind romance, and you've been given a month's leave for honeymoon purposes."

It was more or less what I'd expected after the buildup he'd given the unknown girl—he doesn't pass out words like "competent" lightly—but that didn't make me like it any better.

"All right, I'm a horse," I said. "Who're we stalking and how, playing the honeymoon couple seeing the sights of Europe. It doesn't seem like a very promising gambit to me."

What I really meant, I suppose, was that the matrimonial approach, while it has certain advantages, also has certain drawbacks for the personnel involved. Playing house with a fellow agent of the opposite sex, even a good-looking one, isn't my idea of fun and games. It's hard to act appropriately tender toward a little lady you know can throw you across the room; and I kind of like to have some say about whom I sleep with. However, I didn't tell him this directly. Where a job is concerned, our likes and dislikes are considered quite irrelevant.

Mac ignored my indirect protest, if you could call it that. He said, "Well, there's a casual visit you will make in London. Your motivation will ostensibly be quite innocent, in line with your bridegroom cover, but the mere fact of your contact with a man who is under surveillance will call you to the attention of the other team, or teams. After they have identified you as one of our people, I think we can safely count on nature taking its more or less violent course."

"Teams, plural?" I grimaced. "You sound as if you expected a battle royal over there, sir. How many other outfits do you figure we'll be taking on?"

"At least three, maybe more," he said. "The man in whom we're really interested—not the subsidiary figure you'll see in London—has a fairly large and efficient organization of his own, or it has him. We don't quite know the relationship there. Of course the British are interested, since he is using their country for a base of operations. And of course the Russians are trying to turn the situation to their own advantage."

"Sure," I said. "This base of operations you mentioned, sir. Do we know where it is?"

"If we did, your play-acting would not be necessary. We think we have the area narrowed down to Scotland, probably northwestern Scotland. Your itinerary has been arranged accordingly."

"I'm under the impression that's a rugged country for a honeymoon," I said. "At a hundred and five pounds, my bride's a little light for real tough going."

"Don't worry about Claire. If she can survive the jungles of southeast Asia, she can presumably survive the Scottish Highlands."

"Well, it's not quite the same thing, sir, but I see your point."

"Of course, you can expect to be under very close observation, by one party or another, from the moment you make your first contact in London. You will govern yourselves accordingly."

"Yes, sir," I said. "Once we've tripped the trigger, so to speak, we'll assume we're getting the full treatment: mikes in the room, bugs on the phone, electronic gadgets stuck to the car with Alnico magnets, and little lip-reading men with big binoculars hiding in the bushes. We'll even keep up the act in the john, if you like." I made a face. "Not to mention, I suppose, in bed."

"That will be fine," he said calmly. The facts of life are pretty much taken for granted around that office. He went on: "There is really no doubt that *you* will be spotted, Eric. You are in their files, and in a sense you are expected—you, or someone like you."

I said, "I won't thank you for the compliment, sir, until I'm sure it is one."

"What I mean is," he said, "that it's a matter of record that we've used you as a troubleshooter before, when a job went sour on us. We've just lost the man who was handling this assignment. Actually, he wasn't ours, but we've been asked to replace him. The British authorities are delaying public identification of the body for reasons of their own, but they passed the word in private."

I frowned thoughtfully. "Which brings up a ticklish point, sir. The British authorities. What is the official line?"

Mac said without expression, "Officially, you will cooperate with the British authorities, and give them full respect and consideration."

"Yes, sir," I said. "And unofficially?"

He sighed. "Eric, you are being tiresome. Unofficially, you will of course do the job assigned to you the way it was assigned, regardless of who may attempt to interfere. The British still, apparently, have hopes of accomplishing this mission in a genteel and civilized way. After a number of failures, we have given up such hopes. Do I make myself clear?"

"Yes, sir," I said. "Does this man I'm replacing have a name? I mean, did he have a name?"

"His real name doesn't matter. You didn't know him. He was calling himself Paul Buchanan, posing as an American tourist interested in tracing his Scottish forebears. That is the only lead we have, at present, to the person we are seeking—I'll give you the details in a moment—and Buchanan was working on it. He started, as you will, in London, traveled north to Scotland, and disappeared into the Highlands. He was found dead near a small town called Ullapool, on an inlet of the west coast, pretty far up."

"Dead how?" I asked.

"The preliminary report we have, courtesy of the British, states only that he seems to have died of natural causes." Mac's voice was toneless.

"Sure," I said. "And just what was friend Buchanan doing way to hell and gone up there?"

"We don't know." After a moment Mac frowned. "What do you mean, Eric?"

I said, "To the best of my recollection, that's Mackenzie and MacDonnell territory up there, sir. The Buchanans come from farther south, not much above Glasgow. Why would anyone tracing them take off into the remote western Highlands?"

Mac said, "Maybe that was the mistake that betrayed him. As I told you, he was not one of ours, and I don't know how good a briefing he had, or how good an actor he was. He obviously blundered badly enough, somehow, to get himself caught and killed." Mac eyed me sharply. "And how do you know so much about the families of Scotland? You don't happen to have an ancestor who came from there?"

I shrugged. "I can probably scare one up if he's needed."

"I thought your family was strictly Scandinavian."

It was nice to catch him on something he didn't have in the files. "Whose family is strictly anything?" I asked. "Quite a few Scots migrated to Sweden at one time or another, sir. This was a guy named Glenmore. He had a claymore for hire and times were tough at home, so he went over a few hundred years back to swing his blade for a royal personage named Gustavus Adolphus, who happened to have employment for gents handy with edged weapons. Apparently he married and stayed on after the wars were over. I don't remember the exact date or the place in Scotland he came from, but it's in a pile of stuff I'm paying storage charges on. My mother always claimed we were distantly related to some old Scottish dukes or barons."

"Modest people, the Scots," Mac said dryly. "I never met an Irishman yet who'd admit to being descended from anything less than a king. I want you to dig up as much family information as you can, Eric. It will give you an excuse for following Buchanan's trail through the wilderness of Scottish genealogy."

"Yes, sir," I said. "Let's hope my family tree grows up Ullapool way. If not, I suppose I'll have to bend it slightly. And then what?"

"By that time, I hope, you will have attracted enough attention from enough people to make the next move obvious. What form the attention will take is something we cannot predict. That is why Claire is being assigned to you."

"She's the backup man, or woman?"

"Precisely. She will be the featherheaded little blonde bride—naive, ineffectual, and, we hope, ignored. This will give her an advantageous position from which to make her move when the time comes."

"You mean," I said, "when some natural causes try to make me dead like they did Buchanan?"

"That is more or less what I mean," Mac said slowly. "However, you must remember that Claire's job is not to serve you as bodyguard. The subject is her chief concern. Her assignment is to take care of him after you have, we hope, led him to reveal himself. She is under strict orders not to break cover—not under any circumstances—until she is certain that it will lead directly to the completion of the mission." He paused, looking at me steadily. "I hope I again make myself clear."

"Yes, sir," I said. "You always do, sir. In other words, as far as staying alive is concerned, I'm on my own. Claire will play helpless, letting the bodies fall where they may, until she sees the big break coming. Okay, I'm warned. I won't look to her for protection." I regarded him across the desk. "And now, sir, just what is the mission—or should I say, who is the mission? I've still heard no names and received no descriptions."

He said, as if in answer, "You've had all your shots?"

"Yes, sir. I'm immune to everything but the common cold. Any mosquito or tsetse fly that tries to stick germs into my hide is wasting his cotton-picking time. You'd think I was heading for a tropical-fever belt instead of the

Scottish Highlands. I suppose there's a reason." I studied his face a moment longer. "Could it have some connection with the so-called natural causes that killed Buchanan?"

"It could," he said. "Don't count too much on those shots, Eric. Buchanan had had them, too."

"I see," I said. Again, it wasn't exactly true. "Perhaps you'd better tell me about it, sir," I said.

He did.

2

The information he gave me was very secret, so secret that it was known only to Washington and London, and maybe Moscow, Berlin, Paris, and Peking. Anyway, it was so highly classified that it hadn't been transmitted to Claire, in transit, because Mac didn't have authority to entrust it to an ordinary messenger. I was going to have to give her the final details after we'd met and found a secure place to talk.

Whether or not the dope I'd been given was actually as secret as its classification indicated—very few things are—it gave me plenty to think about on my flight from Washington to New York. I was still thinking about it as I climbed the stairs to the BOAC economy-class waiting room after going through the usual ticket-and-passport routine. I had the description, so I had no trouble spotting my bride. The world isn't exactly crowded with pretty little sunburned blondes, although it would be nice if it were. To clinch the identification, she was reading the current copy of *House Beautiful*, presumably boning up on how to furnish the split-level honeymoon cottage when we got home.

I stopped in front of her. She looked up from her magazine. It was a funny moment. She'd presumably been given as much information about me as I'd been given about her. We knew everything about each other that mattered professionally, and we didn't know each other at all, and now we were under orders to play man and wife—with all that implied—for days, maybe weeks, depending on how the job went.

There was an instant of wary appraisal. I got the impression she wasn't any happier about being told whom to share her bed and toothpaste with than I'd been. Then she went smoothly into her act. She jumped to her feet, letting the magazine fall unheeded to the floor.

"Matt, darling!" she cried, and threw her arms around my neck and kissed me hard, attracting some bored glances from our fellow travelers-to-be. "Oh, I was so afraid your plane was going to be late, dear!" she went on breathlessly. "How was Washington? Did you get your last-minute business all taken care of?"

I nibbled affectionately at her ear. "Sure," I said. "Did you have a nice visit with your folks, honey? I wish I could have gone with you and met them as we'd planned, but we'll stop by when we get back…"

These histrionics were probably unnecessary, since there was no reason to think anybody would be watching us with more than casual interest until I made my first move to follow Buchanan's trail, in London. Still, somebody might check back this far later, and I always feel that if you're going to play a part, you might as well play it all the way, at least in public—and it's hard to tell what's public and what isn't, these electronic days. I was glad to see that Claire had the same professional attitude. I reminded myself that she was no longer Claire to me: she was Winifred Helm, my sweet little wife.

I looked her over and decided that I could have done worse. In fact, she was probably the cutest wife I'd ever had, for pretend or for real. I was married in earnest once, to a tall New England girl—I was a respectable, home-loving citizen for a number of years—but anybody who's been in this line of work is a poor matrimonial risk and it fizzled in the end. Now I had a pretty, phony little spouse, imported from the Orient, who had to stand on tiptoe to kiss me.

Her summer tan—well, it looked like a summer tan, however she'd got it—gave her an air of wholesomeness that was probably more convincing, for the role, than a pink Dresden-doll complexion would have been. That baby-face gag has been pulled a little too often. The warm dark skin also made an attractive contrast to her pale hair and clear blue eyes. She had just the right figure for her diminutive size, by no means sturdy and still not so fragile that you had to worry lest the first breeze carry her away. She was all done up for honeymoon purposes, to use Mac's terminology, in a little blue suit rather scanty in the skirt, a tricky white blouse, little white gloves, and one of those soft ruffled hats or bonnets, kind of resembling big fuzzy bathing caps, that seem to have taken the country by storm.

She looked just like the nice little girl next door, the one you'd like to take to the beach or tennis court, and she'd killed seven times, twice with her bare hands. At least so said the record in Washington, and I had no reason to doubt it. Well, they come in all shapes and sizes: small shapely females as well as tall bony males. I'd been in the business longer than she. I was in no position to criticize her homicidal record.

We held hands clear across the Atlantic. The stewardesses—healthy-looking, friendly British girls who were a pleasant change of pace from the movie queens officiating on American airlines—spotted us as newly-weds immediately, as they were supposed to. They thought my pride was a living doll, but they weren't quite sure she hadn't made a mistake in marrying an older man. However, I seemed to appreciate her, and that inclined them to forgive me my advanced years—I won't say how advanced; I'll just say that neither girl was much over twenty.

Over the ocean, we met the new day traveling westward. The night hadn't lasted more than a few hours, jet travel being what it is. At London's Heathrow Airport, the passport-and-customs bit was rudimentary. Afterwards, a man from Claridge's Hotel descended on us, stuck us in a taxi, and aimed us hotelward.

"Is that all there's to it?" my Winifred asked as we rode through the frantic, left-handed London traffic. I saw that she was genuinely surprised. I guess she'd come from places where border formalities were taken more seriously.

I said, "Unless we decide to visit behind the Iron Curtain, the only time we're likely to have any trouble is when we're getting back into the U.S. Then we can expect to be treated as hardened criminals with evil intentions— although I've heard rumors that even our savage customs watchdogs are on a courtesy kick these days." After a while, I said, "There's where we're staying, honey. Pipe the doorman in top hat and knee breeches."

Winnie played up, looking at first prettily intrigued and then a little dubious, like the naive country bride she was supposed to be. "But isn't it terribly expensive? And… and fancy? My clothes aren't really…"

"Your clothes are swell," I said. "I saved money on the plane tickets so we could blow it here. Everybody ought to stay at Claridge's once. Don't be scared, baby. Hell, they let the queen of Holland stay here all during World War II, and she isn't half as good-looking as you are."

This exchange was probably wasted on the cab driver behind his glass partition, but it warmed us up for our performance inside the hotel. In our best self-conscious-newlywed manner, we ran the gauntlet of polite, formally attired reception clerks—the tailcoat industry would be in a bad way if it lost the trade of European hostelries—and were ushered into a third-floor room large enough so that, if you needed exercise, you could roll back the rug and play handball beyond the bed. After a couple of vigorous games, you could cool off in a tub large enough to swim in. The phone was supplemented by various auxiliary bell systems for summoning waiters, maids, and valets. It was quite a layout, in its quiet, old-fashioned, overstaffed way.

"Gee, it's gorgeous," said my bride, wide-eyed. "But… but can we really afford it, dear?"

I said, "What's money, honey? It isn't every day a man gets married."

I put my arm around her shoulders and gave her a loving hug while passing some British change to the bellboy, who bowed and withdrew. There had been some discussion in Washington as to whether a man, even an experienced agent, embarking on his honeymoon after a brief, breathless courtship, would be foresighted enough to provide himself with foreign currency. It had been decided that he would, if only to impress his sweet little bride with his worldly knowledge.

When the door had closed behind the boy, said sweet little bride twisted free abruptly.

"Jesus Christ!" she said. "Haven't you any sense at all?"

It was a different voice from the shy, birdlike tones she'd been using: deeper and harsher. It took me by surprise.

"What's the matter?"

She touched her upper arm tenderly. "Here every damn horse-doctor south of the Equator has been running six-inch needles into my arms and rump—both rumps—and you've got to go squeezing me like a ripe lime you're about to drop into a nice gin and tonic!" She caught the uneasy glance I threw around the room, and went on irritably: "Oh, hell, relax! Give your profession a rest,

Mr. Helm. I'm just as security-conscious as you are, but if somebody knows enough about us already to have this room bugged waiting for us, our whole act's a big waste of time and you know it. So for now, in here, we can just be ourselves, whoever that is. Sometimes I kind of forget, don't you?"

I knew what she meant, of course. After pretending to be a certain number of other people, you tend to lose track of the person you really are. However, it didn't seem like the moment for a discussion of the psychological hazards of the trade.

"Sorry about your arm," I said. "I wasn't thinking, I guess."

She pulled off her hat, threw it at a chair, and shook out her blonde hair. It was rather short, very fine, and a little mussed and matted now from long confinement. She squirmed out of her little jacket and dropped it on top of the hat. She smoothed her frilly white blouse into her abbreviated blue skirt and drew a long breath.

"God, what a week!" she said. "I don't think I've spent more than a day of it below thirty thousand feet. If I have to strap myself into another airplane seat, I'll go stir-crazy."

I said, "If airplane seats give you claustrophobia, doll, you'll flip twice when you see the car we're getting. It's a real shoehorn job."

"I know," she said. "They told me. One of those lousy little sports cars. Whose bright idea was that?"

"Mine," I said. "I like them, big or little, and I'm the guy who'll be doing most of the driving. And you haven't seen the deer paths they use for roads in this country. I figured we'd better have something small, but fast and agile, just in case. Besides, it's just the kind of flashy car a sophisticated jerk named Helm would buy so he could show off his driving ability to his innocent young bride." I grinned at her. "Hi, Bridie."

She looked up at me for a moment. Then she gave me a funny, crooked little smile in return. I still knew her hardly at all, certainly not well enough to read her mind, but just then I knew in a general way what she was thinking about, because I was thinking about the same thing. I mean, we'd discussed everything from hypodermic injections to automobiles, but there was one subject that remained untouched, and it couldn't be ignored forever.

Winifred sighed, and looked down, and began to unbutton her blouse. I didn't say anything. She looked up again, rather defiantly.

"Well, we'd better get it over with, hadn't we?"

"You call it," I said.

She said, "Hell, we've got a lot of beds to inhabit in the next week or so, and orders are to make the springs creak convincingly. We'd better kind of get acquainted, if you know what I mean, before we have an audience." She walked quickly over to her suitcase, yanked it open, and tossed some fragile white lingerie my way. "Pick the one that arouses the beast in you, Mr. Helm. We can't have the maid seeing the bridal nighties all in mint condition. And for God's sake take it easy. Remember I'm tender practically all over…"

3

It wasn't the most passionate performance of my life. I found it difficult to work up a lot of enthusiasm over the idea of raping a business associate in broad daylight. Still, she was a good-looking and well-constructed kid, her responses were adequate if not spectacular, and biology is a fairly reliable source of motive power. Afterwards we lay close for a while; then she moved away and wiggled around a bit, pulling the various filmy layers of her trousseau nightie straight about her. Having got herself untangled, she sighed and lay still.

"Well," she said, "that's that."

I couldn't help laughing at her matter-of-fact tone. "I've heard more glowing testimonials."

"No doubt," she murmured, "from volunteer partners, Mr. Helm, but you can hardly expect a girl to go wild over the idea of compulsory copulation. Come to that, I didn't notice you behaving as if I were the answer to your erotic prayers."

I grinned. "Maybe we'll improve with practice. Anyway, it's nice to lie in bed after sitting up all night on the plane. We might as well make ourselves comfortable and hold a council of war; we may not have another chance to talk freely for quite a while. Can I get you a drink or cigarette or something?"

"My cigarettes are in my purse, on the dresser... Thanks."

Standing by the bed, I held a match for her, and set an ashtray on the little table beside her. There was something pleasantly illicit about loafing around a luxurious hotel room in pajamas in the middle of the day with a pretty girl for company, even if she did know judo and karate and could keep all her shots inside the critical ones of a man-sized target at combat ranges. I decided that our romantic interlude, for all its shortcomings, had served a useful purpose. Certainly it had averted a lot of the strains and frustrations that would inevitably have developed had we tried to fake the essential man-wife relationship indefinitely.

Standing there, I looked down at my pint-sized partner thoughtfully. Her eyes were very blue against her brown skin, which in turn looked smooth and warm against the pale hair and white nightie.

She blew smoke up at me and said, "Cut it out, Helm."

"Cut what out?"

"Don't be a sentimental slob. You're standing there willing yourself to like me, aren't you? Maybe even fall in love with me a little, for God's sake! Just because we've made a little sex together—and rather badly, at that—

you feel obliged to tell yourself how cute the wittle girl looks in the gweat big bed. Well, pour yourself a drink or something and stop romanticizing. Remember that any resemblance between us and a pair of lovebirds is strictly phony. We're just a couple of hired clowns practicing our vaudeville turn."

She was right, of course. I grinned and got back into bed beside her, pulled up the covers, and arranged some pillows behind us.

"Sure," I said. "Now if you're quite through putting me in my place, maybe we can discuss some matters of real importance."

She turned to look at me, a little startled. After a moment she laughed. "I'm sorry, I didn't mean... well, maybe I did. Matters of importance like what?"

"Like a guy named Buchanan, who's dead. And a guy named McRow, who isn't, but you're supposed to correct that unfortunate condition at your earliest convenience. Always assuming that somehow we can manage to locate Dr. McRow and bring you within effective range of him."

She frowned. "McRow. They wouldn't tell me. It was a big secret. They just gave me the general background of the job. McRow. I never heard of him. McRow." She tasted the sound of it. "First name?"

"Archibald," I said. "It doesn't seem quite fair, does it?"

"What do you mean?"

"A poor guy saddled with a name like Archibald would seem to have troubles enough already without having nasty characters like us gunning for him."

Winnie didn't smile. Well, maybe it wasn't very funny. She said curtly, "Description?"

"Forty-seven, five-seven, one-ninety."

"A middle-aged butterball," she murmured.

"That's right. Short and chubby. Round face. Dark hair combed to cover a bald patch. Brown eyes, somewhat myopic, corrected with gold-rimmed glasses. Small hands and feet. Clean-shaven when he bothers to shave, but he's apt to neglect such minor details when in the grip of scientific enthusiasm, and I gather he gets gripped fairly often. Clothes generally shabby, adorned with acid burns and other chemical decorations. Lots of brains and a terrible character, they say. He can't get along with anybody, and nobody can get along with him. He sees himself as the only intelligent person in a world full of morons, all of whom are trying to take advantage of his genius."

"Are they?"

"Well, sure. Isn't that what genius is for?" I asked. "He worked for a big drug company first. They made a mint off one of his discoveries—some fancy antibiotic—and he just got his salary and a small bonus. That was the way his contract read. Then he got himself a new contract and dug up some other stuff that was interesting and potentially lucrative, only without knowing it he'd kind of crossed the fence into fields that were being cultivated by the government for military purposes. Suddenly he found himself working for the biological warfare boys under very strict security, still making no more than a lousy four-figure salary—well, maybe five by this time—and he's a man, we're told, who likes to dream in millions. Don't for a minute get Archie mixed up with your idealistic, scientific dreamers, doll. His fantasies, sleeping or waking, seem to deal mainly with dough."

"Go on."

"With this attitude, it was only natural," I said, "that when somebody came along and waved some real cash under his nose, he grabbed it and vanished. He left behind a note saying that the Fourteenth Amendment had abolished slavery and nobody had the right to tell him where to work or for how much. He also intimated that there was no need for the U.S. authorities to worry about his compromising their silly security in any way, since neither he nor his new sponsors had the slightest interest in the childish and obsolete stuff the government people had had him on. He had much more fascinating projects in mind. Under the circumstances, he wrote, he saw no reason why his departure should be the subject of any official concern whatever, and he would resent, strongly, any further interference in his affairs." I shrugged. "In a way, you can see his point. After all, it's his brain and it seems to be a pretty good one. You can hardly blame him for wanting to cash in on it."

Winnie said coolly, "It isn't our business to see people's points, Mr. Helm."

I glanced at her sideways, and moved my shoulders slightly. There had been a few moments when we'd been practically human together; perhaps it was just as well we were getting away from that. If she wanted to take a tough and humorless attitude toward the work—well, it's generally considered pretty tough and humorless work.

I said, "You may call me Matt. Incredible though it may seem, wives do address their husbands with such disrespectful familiarity these decadent days."

She said, still unsmiling, "I don't suppose the government paid much attention to Dr. McRow's warning, Matt."

I said, "Hell, you know those Washington bureaucrats, Winnie. They didn't even realize it was a serious warning. They were so impressed with their own importance that it simply didn't occur to them that one chubby little man with glasses would have the nerve to warn them off— them, and the United States of America. They went after him." I grimaced. "That is to say, they sent people after him. Despite the note, they decided that he was endangering the national security, or something."

"What happened?"

"Nothing much," I said, "at first. They had a hell of a time locating him. Then, after several months, an agent picked up some kind of a trail out west in the California mountains. Shortly thereafter, said agent disappeared. A little while later he reappeared, dead. He'd apparently contracted a severe case of measles while he was missing."

"Measles? You don't die of measles."

I said dryly, "It kind of depends on the measles. And on the natural immunity of the subject. There are cases on record of primitive tribes wiped out by ordinary measles, when they made contact with civilization. Apparently, since he vanished, Archie has developed a private brand that affects civilized people the same way. He was thoughtful enough to have a warning sign pinned to the infected body, or California might have had a nasty epidemic."

Winnie said, "That sounds like grandstanding to me."

"Not only to you," I said. "The idea has occurred to others. Anyway, investigation of the area turned up a deserted building that had been used as a lab—quite an elaborate setup, as a matter of fact—but it was stripped and deserted. McRow's sponsors, whoever they are, had had time to move their genius and his operation elsewhere. The next time he was spotted, he had a place up in the Andes, but again the agent who picked up the trail managed to stick his neck in a noose before he could pinpoint the location. This one died of chicken pox. And don't tell me you don't die of chicken pox, doll. The agent's health record even showed he'd had a severe case as a child, but Archie's trained bugs paid no attention to his built-in immunity. They killed him dead."

Winnie frowned thoughtfully. "In other words, the man has found a way of increasing the virulence somehow."

"In non-technical terms, that's about it," I said. "Which brings up the interesting question: What happens when he stops playing around with children's diseases and applies his method to something really gruesome, like smallpox or cholera. He's building up to something, obviously. He could have had those agents shot or tossed off a cliff. Instead, he's been passing out samples, deliberately showing us and the rest of the world what he can do.

Where does he go from here? And just who are the people helping him and what are their motives? Those are the questions bugging the big boys in Washington. The fact that the same questions are probably being considered in Moscow and elsewhere doesn't help their peace of mind one little bit."

"Are we sure it isn't Moscow that's giving McRow aid and comfort?"

"Sure?" I said. "Who's sure of anything? All we know is that they seem to be just as baffled as we are. And that whoever is sheltering Archie has plenty of money and manpower, but he doesn't seem particularly anxious to take up residence in the workers' homeland."

Winnie hesitated. "If this were a movie, I'd suggest an international mastermind of crime who was hoping to blackmail the world with the ultimate biological weapon."

"Don't think that possibility isn't being considered quite seriously," I said. "But in the absence of any clues to the identity of McRow's current patrons, Washington is just assuming they aren't driven by philanthropic motives. And after three abortive tries to take McRow undamaged, including Buchanan's, well, much as they'd like to have the big brain back working for democracy... Anyway, it was decided as a last resort to give us the job. We're supposed to take care of it before Archie finishes whatever it is he's really working on; also before anybody else gets hold of him, including our friends the British. The only trouble is, nobody has any notion what his target date may be. It could be tomorrow. Or it could be yesterday." I sighed regretfully and reached for the phone. "Well, this has been real pleasant, ma'am, but we've got work to do."

"Who're you calling?"

"I'm supposed to start the ball rolling, so to speak, by making a date with a certain genealogist."

"A certain what?"

"A gent who draws family trees," I said. "Dr. McRow, fortunately, has two weaknesses. One, as I've said, is money. The other is ancestors. He apparently started life without any, except the usual connection with Adam and Eve. In the U.S. he was born on the wrong side of the tracks, socially as well as financially, but after coming to Scotland he apparently got the notion that his family had once been big and important there. That's how the trail was picked up again after being lost over in South America. He'd sent in his name—it had to be his real name, of course—to an ancestor-hunting outfit here in London. He'd hired them to prove a connection, however dim and distant, between his branch of the McRow family and some fine old Highland clan. For a man in hiding, it was a crazy breach of security, but then there's no real proof the guy's rational outside the laboratory. Anyway, this is where Buchanan started, and we're supposed to kind of follow in his footsteps until we hit a better lead… Shhh, here we go."

The switchboard had got me the number. A man who identified himself as Ernest Walling, of Simpson and Walling, was asking my identity and business. I gave the true name and the false story—the yarn about wanting to trace my own ancestors that we'd cooked up for the purpose. After I'd finished, Walling was silent for a little, presumably digesting the information.

"Ah, I see," he said presently. "Would it be convenient for you to come here at four o'clock, Mr. Helm? That will give me time to do a little preliminary research, and I will be able to say more definitely whether or not I can help you."

"Four would be fine."

He hesitated again. "Ah, you say you are staying at Claridge's? And you are from America?"

"That's right."

"You wouldn't happen to know an American gentleman named Buchanan, Paul Buchanan?"

I laughed. "America is a big place, Mr. Walling. I'm afraid I don't know any Buchanans."

"No, of course not. He called on us recently and I just wondered… I will be glad to see you at four, Mr. Helm. Thank you for calling."

I put down the phone, frowning. "He mentioned Buchanan," I said to Winnie. "That could mean something, but I'll be damned if I know what."

"At this stage of the game, one hardly ever knows what," she said. "Damn it, I'm stuck. Give me a hand, will you?"

She'd got out of bed, and she'd started pulling her nightie off over her head, forgetting to untie the flowing sash beforehand, and now she couldn't reach it. I yanked one end of the bow and it came loose. She emerged from the lingerie quite unselfconsciously, revealing a nice little body, brown practically all over—but I noticed that she had got too much sun on the back and shoulders. They had peeled badly, not too long ago. Subsequent careful exposure to sun or a sunlamp had almost restored the uniform brown pigmentation, but not quite. Looking closely at her face as she turned, I now saw similar traces in her nose, masked by makeup.

It happens to lots of girls who try to do all their tanning on the first day of vacation. It wasn't out of character for the role she was playing, but I had a hunch the burns had not been the result of loafing too long on a South Seas beach, drink in hand. She'd apparently had a rough time out there. Well, it was none of my business.

"Well, we're committed," I said. "If the Simpson-Walling phone is tapped, or the office is wired for sound, as Washington seems to think, somebody's already checking on a gent named Helm, staying at Claridge's. We can expect the hostile eyes and ears to focus on us any minute."

She grimaced. "You don't have to tell me. I hope you're not one of the men in whom sex is followed by acute starvation. I'd like to try out that oversized bathtub before we have lunch." She slipped off her tiny wristwatch and looked at it before putting it on the dresser. "The date's for four? It's only noon now. That gives us plenty of time."

"Us?" I said. She glanced at me quickly. I said, "I don't really think you ought to be contaminated by any contact with Simpson and Walling, sweetheart. You're little Kid

Innocence, remember? Let's keep you that way."

She hesitated, and said reluctantly, "I guess you're right. Okay, I stay. Matt?"

"Yes?"

"You didn't tell me what Buchanan died of."

"Bubonic plague," I said. "Also known as the Black Death. A fine upstanding adult disease for a change."

She whistled softly and said, "This McRow character. He sounds kind of crazy all around. Delusions of grandeur and stuff."

She looked cute standing there without anything on, but it was my chance to turn the tough-and-humorless treatment on her, and I wasn't about to pass it up.

I said, "It's not our business to psychoanalyze him, doll. All we're required to do is kill him."

4

After lunch, which we had served in the room, I called a car dealer on Berkeley Square; then I left Winnie to take a nap while I went over to pick up our transportation: a gaudy, bright red Triumph Spitfire sports job, the last car in the world an agent on a secret mission would choose to drive. Well, that was the idea.

It had sixty-seven horsepower, an eighty-three-inch wheelbase, a top speed of ninety-something, and a turning circle of twenty-four feet, which meant that if you got just a little gay with the wheel, you'd find yourself going back the way you came. This was why I'd picked it. In a land of fast drivers and unlimited highway speeds I wasn't likely to be able to equip myself to outrun the opposition—considering the departmental budget—but in this little bomb, if need be, I might out-dodge it.

They sent me out to a garage at the edge of town for the actual delivery, and by the time I'd picked my way back to the hotel, creeping timidly down the left side of

the street while the crazy traffic swirled around me, it was
well after three. I turned my miniature hotrod over to the
doorman and went up to the room. Winnie was sitting on
the bed with a bunch of pillows behind her, reading the
London papers provided by the management.

"Mission accomplished?" she asked.

"I got it here," I said. "But this is no place to learn a
new way of driving. I'll be glad when we're safely out in
the country. God, what a rat-race!"

She laughed. She was wearing a sleeveless, beltless
white linen dress, I noticed, that looked as if you could
have made it with one hand out of an old bedsheet. I must
say I prefer my women with waistlines, but the absurdly
simple little tube of a garment made her look very young
and innocent indeed. It was hard to keep in mind that she
was well over twenty, nearer twenty-five, and that she'd
killed seven men and would, we hoped, soon raise her
score to eight.

She'd left her shoes off for comfort. Her knees-up
reading position didn't leave many secrets under the
brief dress, but then, we were supposed to be married. I
reached over the end of the bed and pinched her big toe
through her stocking.

"Well, I'll see you in an hour or so," I said.

"You're off again?"

"I just wanted to get rid of that damn car before I
cracked it up. I'll take a cab from here."

She said, just a little too casually perhaps, "Well, toss
me my cigarettes while you're up."

I grinned. "Don't give me that while-you're-up routine, small fry. This is a high-class joint. Around here we got manners. We say please."

"Please."

I dropped the cigarettes and matches in her lap and moved to the door. "Don't be lonely while I'm gone." She hesitated. "Matt, do you think it's tactically okay if I go out and do a little rubbernecking and window-shopping? I've never seen London, you know."

She was a funny mixture of professional ruthlessness and girlish curiosity. I didn't like to disappoint her, and I certainly didn't want her to think I was pulling rank and seniority on her, but I said, "I'd rather you wouldn't. The situation could go critical on us any time. If you don't mind, I'd like you to stay right here."

Her blue eyes looked very cold for a moment. "And if I do mind?"

"Then go the hell out and rubberneck, but you'd better wrap up good. That's not much dress you've got on and it looks like rain."

"Aren't you being a little stuffy? I didn't come on this job to be kept on ice."

"Of course you did," I said. "You're my delicate darling, and I wouldn't dream of letting you go out there and get your pretty little feet wet. On a different level, I'm supposed to take real good care of you, so you'll be in perfect condition when the time comes for you to slit a man's throat."

She sighed. "All right. You win again. I'll stay, damn

you. Under protest, but I'll stay."

"Thanks."

As I reached for the door again, she said quickly, "Matt, wait."

I looked back. She'd swung her legs off the bed. She paused to stick her feet into her shoes, not so much for protection, I gathered—it was a deep, soft rug—as for the extra two or three inches the high heels gave her. She came over and deliberately put her arms around my neck and rose on tiptoe to kiss me on the mouth.

"There," she said. "You can be wiping off the lipstick, husband-like, as you go down the hall."

"Sure."

There was a little pause. I was tempted to add something mushy to the effect that she was a pretty nice kid, after all, and working with her wasn't going to be quite the ordeal I'd expected. While I struggled with the impulse, the telephone rang, which was just as well. I mean, this buddy-buddy stuff may be all right in the armed forces, but in our line of work you're much better off hating your partner's guts. Then you won't feel so bad if he breaks a leg and you have to shoot him—and if you think that's just a figure of speech, Buster, I envy you the happy TV world you live in.

Winnie had gone over to pick up the phone. "Hello," she said. Her voice was suddenly thin and sweet and rather timid. "Yes, this is… this is Mrs. Helm. Yes, he's right here. Yes, of course. Just a moment."

She held out the phone with a little shrug to indicate

that she had no idea who was calling. I took it and said, "Helm here."

A very British voice said, "Crowe-Barham. I assumed it wasn't undiplomatic to telephone you, old chap, since you were registered under your own name." He waited for me to say something. When I didn't, he went on: "If your memory falters, the given names are Leslie Alastair, and the joint operation was called Adder. Why do they have this awful compulsion to name them after reptiles, I wonder. You will recall that it was rather a sticky affair. I still owe you a drink, maybe a trifle more, depending on the going rate for slightly shopworn baronets, so I asked Colonel Stark, my current superior—I don't think you know him—for permission to get in touch with you. Are you in our city on business, and if so can we be of assistance? Her Majesty's troops are at your service."

"No business," I said, remembering my instructions. I wasn't supposed to break cover for anybody if I could help it, certainly not an unidentified voice on the phone. The fact that I was fairly sure I recognized the voice made no real difference. The accent is easy to imitate, and there are a lot of good mimics around. I went on: "I'm on my honeymoon, *amigo*, and I don't need any help from the troops, thanks."

"Congratulations, old fellow. I'm sure from her voice that the lady is perfectly charming." He hesitated, and went on with a diffident stubbornness: "You're quite certain there's nothing I can do."

I said, "Under the circumstances, that could be

parlayed into an off-color joke."

"What?" He chuckled at the other end of the line. "Oh, quite. Unintentional, I assure you."

"How did you know I was here?"

"We do try to keep track of the more prominent visitors to our fair island, old boy."

"Sure," I said. "Prominent."

"I gather from your address that accommodations are no problem, but what about transportation? If you have no car, I would be happy to put one at your disposal. A small Rolls-Royce? A well-mannered 3.8 Jaguar? Take your pick, but may I be so bold as to suggest a chauffeur until you become accustomed once more to our perverse left-handed traffic?"

I hesitated, but his persistence indicated that I wasn't going to get rid of him by phone. It seemed best to meet the situation head on, and I said, "As a matter of fact, I've just picked up a car and had a taste of your traffic and I don't want any more at the moment... Okay, I never pass up a chance to travel first-class. I'll take you up on that chauffeur-driven Rolls, if you can get it here in time to make a four-o'clock appointment across town."

"Very good," he said. "The auto will be in front of your hotel in ten minutes. Cheerio."

The telephone went dead. I took it from my ear and made a face at it before putting it down. Winnie was waiting for an explanation. I said, "That claimed to be a gent known as Sir Leslie Alastair Crowe-Barham, and from the voice I think it really was. It looks as if my phone call to that genealogical character is beginning to bring in results, although so far you could hardly call them profitable results. The trouble with operating in a friendly country is getting along with their people. Well, I'll do my best to convince him I'm just a blissful bridegroom. That'll put the least strain on international diplomacy."

"He's British Intelligence?" Winnie frowned quickly. "Wait a minute. Crowe-Barham. Not Intelligence, one of the other branches. They had him working out of Hong Kong for a while, didn't they?"

I shrugged. "They may have. I think he mentioned being born out that way, which would make him a logical candidate. I haven't really kept track of him. We worked together just once, several years ago. Now he claims he's being nice to me because I saved his life."

"Did you?"

I shrugged again. "I suppose so. So what? I'd brought him a long way, and I needed him alive, not dead; why should I let him be killed when I could prevent it by pulling a trigger? It was strictly impersonal on my part, and he knows it. He knows damn well he owes me nothing beyond a drink for good marksmanship, but right now, apparently, he thinks it advisable to profess undying gratitude. I guess he wants an excuse to keep a friendly eye on me. After all, it's his country we're playing games in. Did you ever meet him out East?"

Winnie shook her head. "No. You'd better give me a description, in case I should bump into him at a critical moment."

"Sure," I said. "Five eleven, a hundred and fifty—give or take five, reddish hair, gray eyes, a small military moustache. He'd be about thirty now, and he could have put on a little weight, but that languid British type generally doesn't. I never saw him with a monocle, but it would suit him fine." I grimaced. "He was really a pretty good boy—plenty of guts and stamina—but he nearly drove me crazy. I mean, he had a head full of notions about what was brave and what wasn't, as if anybody gave a damn; and his idiot theories about sportsmanship almost got him killed and a lot of other people with him. You know the kind of dope who won't shoot a sitting duck or a standing deer or man with his back turned—as if murder is less reprehensible if the victim is facing north rather than south, or vice versa. Of course he got a lot of that kid stuff knocked out of him on the job, and he's probably outgrown the rest, if he's still in the business, as he seems to be."

"And you feel sure he got in touch with you because of your call to Simpson and Walling?"

I moved my shoulders a bit. "Well, he implied that my name just kind of popped out of a routine checklist of incoming VIP's, but I've been in London three times since Adder, and he's never felt obliged to offer me a Rolls before, or even call up and say hello. Maybe I'll know more after I take this dry-land luxury cruise. Five will get you twenty I'll have the most aristocratic chauffeur in town."

Winnie was frowning dubiously. "Well, be careful," she said. "At least until you check him out. I mean, just because a man was okay yesterday doesn't mean he's okay today, and the British make some funny security slips from time to time."

I reached around to give her a slap in the appropriate place. "Yes, ma'am. Any other advice or instructions, ma'am? Us young operatives sure do appreciate experienced leadership, ma'am."

She rubbed her behind through the little white shift and grinned at me. "All right, grandpa. Be a genius on your own. Just don't play with any strange germs."

"Check," I said. "And if you see a virile virus coming your way, you run like hell."

I walked downstairs, since we were only on the third floor—the second, by the European way of counting floors, which starts one story in the air. When I reached the front door, a taxi was just unloading a rather plump, smartly dressed woman with a lot of furs and stacks of matched airplane luggage. She swept inside without condescending to notice me standing there. I turned to look after her, keeping my glance low—just the usual, casual male appraisal of a pair of receding ankles. Although the lady was a bit too well-upholstered for my taste, the ankles weren't half bad. In fact, they were damn good. Well, I'd known they would be. I'd met them before.

The doorman was offering me the empty cab. Even if I hadn't been expecting more luxurious transportation, I wouldn't have got into that particular taxi. It had pulled up just a little too coincidentally, and I knew a little too much about the woman who'd just got out of it, and maybe I wasn't supposed to recognize her with brown hair and a padded girdle. She'd been blonde when I'd last seen her, and her figure had been considerably less generous, although she'd never been exactly what you'd call a skinny girl.

A silvery Rolls-Royce glided to the curb in front of me as the taxi pulled away. I'd guessed right about the driver. The face under the chauffeur's cap was lean and sported a small reddish moustache. We drew away from the hotel in dignified silence. With its rich leather upholstery and velvety ride, it was an impressive vehicle, although you might have found it a little cramped if you'd been brought up on Cadillacs: the Rolls isn't really a big car.

I said, "That cap looks real good on you, *amigo*."

Sir Leslie Crowe-Barham said without turning his head, "You recognized the lady, of course."

"Probably better than you," I said. "Vadya and I had a lot of fun together down in Arizona and Mexico not so long ago. She's quite a girl. I'd rather have a cobra loose around the place." I grimaced. "Particularly when I'm on my honeymoon."

"Quite. If you've got a four-o'clock appointment, we'd better hurry, old chap. Where can I take you?"

"Wilmot Square," I said. "124 Wilmot Square."

Of course he knew damn well where I was going, having undoubtedly listened in on my phone call to Walling, but he wasn't admitting to any such ungentlemanly shenanigans, any more than I was admitting to being anything but the doting husband of a sweet young bride.

5

Simpson and Walling's offices were in an old stone building without an elevator. A dusty sign informed me that I wanted the fourth floor, and I started up the dark stairs. Nobody jumped at me from the shadows with knife, blackjack, or garotte; nobody shot at me with pistol, crossbow, or blowgun; but it was the kind of place where exotic possibilities came to mind. I couldn't help remembering Mac's words: *You are the stalking-horse.* I was here to attract attention. It didn't have to take the form of seductive ladies in mink or more or less friendly agents in silvery Rolls-Royce cars. It could come as just a plain old bullet in the back.

I stopped in front of the door with the correct legend—SIMPSON AND WALLING, GENEALOGISTS—and paused to catch my breath. There was a button made for pushing, and I pushed it. Footsteps approached the door, which opened cautiously to reveal a thin, sandy, tweedy man with a thin, sandy moustache and pale, nervous eyes of an indeterminate slaty color.

"Mr. Walling?" I said. "I'm Matthew Helm. I called you earlier."

"Oh," he said. "Oh, yes. Do come in, Mr. Helm."

I stepped into a large, untidy room littered with books. There were books on the big table, books on the desk in the corner, and books on the floor, as well as on the shelves along the wall. Mostly they were impressive tomes, hefty enough so that it would take a strong and determined man to think of curling up with one for an evening's quiet reading.

"You must excuse the appearance of the place, sir," Walling said. "Since the accident to my associate, I have been, you know, rather swamped with work. In here, if you please."

He opened the door to an inner office, showed me a wooden armchair, and went behind the desk and sat down. This room was small, and seemed crowded by the few pieces of oak furniture and the two glass-fronted shelves holding more books. The window behind Walling gave me a view of roofs and chimney-pots, wet with rain. I wasn't thinking about the weather, however. I was experiencing the professional annoyance that comes with learning that your briefing has been incomplete in one area and may therefore be in others. Well, that's what happens when you come late on a job and have to depend on other organizations for your information.

"Your partner had an accident?" I said. "I am sorry to hear it, Mr. Walling. I hope it wasn't serious."

Walling gave me a suspicious look, as if he thought I was indulging in irony at his expense, or the missing Simpson's.

"He was killed, Mr. Helm. He was run over by a lorry and killed. Five days ago. I… I am very much upset by his death, as you can imagine. Very much upset. And now the office girl has been taken ill…" He clasped his hands together to keep them from wandering around nervously, as they seemed to have a tendency to do. "But I am boring you with my troubles, sir. You are from America, you said?"

"That's right."

"And you have reason to believe you have illustrious connections in Scotland? You would like us to trace them for you?" Suddenly his tone was sharp, almost sarcastic.

I said, "That's right, Mr. Walling."

He said in the same sharp, scornful voice: "I presume you want a handsome family tree to hang on the wall, complete with coat of arms, showing your relationship to the present Duke of Glenmore. You did say Glenmore over the telephone, did you not?"

He was making it fairly clear that he thought I was a phony, in one way or another. A little salesmanship was in order, and I said smoothly, "Yes, but I don't give a damn about the present duke, Mr. Walling. I didn't even know there was one. As I told you on the phone, it's an earl we seem to be connected with, a long time back. Robert Glenmore, Earl of Dalbright, if that's the proper way to say it. He had two sons, Robert and Edward, in that order. Robert stayed in Scotland as far as I know. Being the oldest, I guess he had something to inherit if he stayed. Edward went to Sweden by way of Germany some time around 1631. He married over there and had kids, who married and had kids, and so forth, until my mother came along. She married, went to the U.S. and had me. I've got all that." I took a long envelope from my inside jacket pocket and laid it on the desk between us. "That's all in here: photostats of the family Bible and other stuff. It's what happened before Robert and Edward and their noble papa that I'd kind of like to find out about."

"Yes, of course." Walling's voice was a little warmer than it had been, but his look was still cold and suspicious. "May I see?"

"That's what I brought it for."

He took out the papers and examined them carefully. I had a sudden, funny impulse to snatch them out of his hand and say to hell with the whole business. I mean, I don't particularly hold with ancestor-worship, but this stuff had meant something to my mother, and I was using it to play dirty games with. I could have had the research department cook me up a set of documents under the name of Ross or Sinclair or McTavish that would have served just as well. Maybe.

Walling said abruptly, "Excuse me just a moment."

He rose and went into the outer room. I heard him opening and closing books out there. I reached for the newspaper I saw on the desk, perhaps just to kill time, perhaps because I saw that it was folded to an inside page on which an item had been encircled—and a name underlined—with red crayon. I wasn't there to make like a detective, of course, but the habit dies hard. It was a short piece from Scotland. The heading read:

MAN FOUND DEAD IN ULLAPOOL MYSTERY

The name that had been underlined was that of my predecessor, Buchanan, described as an American tourist. Apparently the British authorities had let the story out at last. It told me nothing I hadn't known before reading it, except that the body had been found by a London doctor on a walking tour. The death was attributed to natural causes but the authorities were puzzled to account for a sick man's getting himself so far out on a lonely moor. The nature of the disease was not mentioned.

I heard Walling returning, and tossed the paper casually back on the desk, letting him see me do it and think whatever he liked. He glanced from me to the paper and back again as he sat down, but he did not comment.

Instead he said, "My apologies, Mr. Helm."

"For what?"

He regarded me steadily across the desk. I hadn't been impressed with him at first glance, but he was growing on me: he wasn't a fool. The nervous mannerisms that had thrown me off were due, I decided, quite simply to his being scared, and that was understandable. His partner had died. A recent client had died. His secretary had come down sick. Death and disease were striking all around him. In his place I'd have been scared, too.

He said deliberately, "People sometimes come in here and try to pull our legs, Mr. Helm." His voice was expressionless, but he left a little pause in case I wanted to squirm or look away guiltily. I didn't. He went on: "For one reason or another they would like us to supply them with authenticated sets of aristocratic ancestors. Sometimes they try to mislead us with false information. Sometimes they just offer us a handsome fee—perhaps I should say bribe—to 'discover' that blue blood flows in their veins. And of course there are so-called genealogists who accept such commissions." He laughed shortly. "If you had said your mother's name was Lewis and you wanted to trace the honest Welsh coal miners from whom she was descended, I would have received you more cordially, but in this line of work, Mr. Helm, one develops an instinctive mistrust of anyone—particularly, if you'll pardon my saying so, anyone from overseas—who claims to be related to a family of importance. Why, just recently we received by post a rather munificent check from an American named McRow, who wished us to prove that he was descended from the chiefs of the ancient clan McRue." He was watching me as he said it.

"McRue," I said. "That's a new one on me. I've heard of the Scottish McRaes and the Irish McGrews, but never McRue."

"It's an older form of the same name. That branch of the family was wiped out in a feud over two hundred years ago—unless this American McRow actually is a direct descendant, as he claims."

"You couldn't confirm it?"

"My associate was working on it when he died. I haven't had an opportunity to study his results. As I say, I have been very busy." Walling shrugged, still watching me carefully. "And then there was another American who called himself Buchanan. I handled that myself. I'm afraid I was not very polite. He was so obviously an impostor."

I said, "Is that the man in the piece you've got marked in the paper I was just looking at? You mentioned him on the phone."

"Yes, the fellow seems to have contracted some kind of fatal illness up north. Naturally, I was interested, since I talked with him in this office not very long ago."

"And you think he was a phony?"

Walling moved his shoulders minutely. "One should speak no ill of the dead, of course, but I rather doubt the chap's name was even Buchanan. At the time, as I said, I was rather annoyed. His clumsy approach was an insult to the profession. I do not say we cannot be misled, but we like to have it done with a certain amount of finesse."

It was time for a show of indignation, and I said, "Look here, if you're hinting that I'm a fake, too—"

"No. That is why I apologized, Mr. Helm. All your family information—in sharp contrast to Mr. Buchanan's—seems to be absolutely correct. Of course, without seeing your birth certificate and other evidence, I cannot be sure that the family you claim is actually yours, can I? But at least you have presented me with genuine data bearing on a genuine problem in my field, and I appreciate the courtesy."

I reflected that it was just as well, after all, that I had not tried to deceive this sharpie with forged documents. I said hopefully, "Then you'll take the job?"

"No."

"But—"

"Let me explain, sir." His hands got hold of each other again, as if to make sure they wouldn't escape. "Your information is correct and fairly complete. It traces your maternal line back to the early seventeenth century. In other words, you already know what people usually employ a genealogist to find out. You are asking me to start where I would usually finish, and I cannot do it. What you want done is either too hard or much too easy."

"Just what does that mean?"

He looked up from his interlocked fingers and spoke as if he were lecturing a class of backward students: "The official registration of births, deaths, and marriages did not begin in Scotland until 1855, two hundred-odd years later than the period in which you are interested. Earlier, we must depend on the parish records and other documents that may have survived. I have just checked the status of the parish records of Dalbright. They are at present in the Register House in Edinburgh, and unlike some they are fairly complete, but they go back only to 1738. Beyond that—" He shrugged. "It is anybody's guess what diligent research could turn up. My own feeling is that it would be a waste of your time and money, sir. I doubt that you are interested in research for its own sake, and with respect to the more prominent families of Scotland, the basic work has already been done and is readily available to anyone who can read."

"Where?" I asked.

"Sir J.B. Paul's *Scots Peerage* gives the Glenmore history as far back as a certain Norman gentleman, Hugh Fitzwilliam de Clenemar, who was awarded lands in Scotland in 1278. You look surprised, Mr. Helm. You did not know that many of the old Scots names are of Norman origin? It is true. Sinclair, for instance, was originally St. Clair. And Robert the Bruce was descended from a Robert de Brus. Similarly, de Clenemar became Glenmore." Walling grimaced at his clasped hands. "I could, of course, have taken your money and copied the information out of the book and presented it to you, with a flourish, as the result of weeks of laborious research. Instead, I just give you the reference. *The Scots Peerage*, Volume III. You can find a set in any large library. I would lend you our copy, but we do not like to let our books leave the premises, and I am about to close up and go home for the day." He unwound his hands and placed them flat on the desk, preparing to rise. "I hope that is satisfactory, Mr. Helm."

"Why, sure," I said. "I mean, I appreciate your help, Mr. Walling, and I'll go after that book. You're sure I can't... I mean I'd like to pay you for your trouble."

He shoved himself to his feet as if he had to lift a lot more weight than he actually possessed. "It was no trouble, no trouble at all. Incidentally, you will be interested to learn that one of your collateral ancestors, a later Hugh Glenmore, acted as a spy for the Stuarts—that romantic Prince Charlie of whom you may have heard. He was caught and beheaded for his pains. Well, the work of a secret agent has always been a dirty and dangerous business, hasn't it, Mr. Helm?"

"So they tell me," I said, rising to face him.

We stood like that for a moment. I reached out and retrieved my papers and put them away while he watched. His expression wasn't exactly hostile, but it wasn't friendly, either. He was making some allowances for me. He was giving me the benefit of the doubt, Glenmore-wise. The family information I'd shown him had been accurate. He'd liked that. He was willing to assume it really applied to me. However, as far as my business here was concerned, he wasn't fooled for a minute. He knew that, whoever my ancestors might have been, I was no casual tourist.

He drew a long breath. "If you'll wait just a moment, Mr. Helm, I'll walk down with you."

"Sure."

I stood in the outer office while he got his hat and coat. He ushered me out to the stair landing and paused briefly to lock the door behind us. As we descended the stairs, a small, slant-eyed, furtive-looking man in a pulled-down cap and buttoned-up trench coat emerged from a third-floor doorway marked ORIENTAL EXPORTS LTD. He glanced our way, and scuttled downstairs ahead of us.

It was very neatly done. I mean, they had me

sandwiched between them. Suddenly the sinister little man ahead swung around in a threatening manner. While I had my eyes on the big, bright knife that had appeared in his hand, Walling blackjacked me from behind.

6

At least that was the way it was supposed to work. As I say, it was very neat—a little too neat. I've been in the business a reasonable length of time, and when somebody flaunts a junior-grade Fu Manchu under my nose, complete with slant eyes, furtive manner, and gleaming knife, I can't help wondering just what's supposed to hit me from elsewhere while I'm watching the Oriental menace going through the motions.

After all, I'm six feet four inches tall, and for a guy a foot shorter, four or five steps below me on a steep stairway, to do me any immediate damage, he's going to need a pogo stick—or lots of help. There had to be another element involved to make this a reasonable trap, and since there were only three of us present, that element had to be the gent above and behind me, however unlikely a candidate he might appear to be.

As the man below me turned, I brought my hand out of my pants pocket, flipped open my own little folding knife—which I keep in my hand whenever the situation looks doubtful—and pivoted sharply, ducking low and driving the blade up and back. If I was wrong, I was going to have some awkward explanations to make, but that decision is one I made long ago. The only death I'm not prepared to explain is my own.

I wasn't wrong. The whistling sap—I guess they call it a cosh in England—told me as much, as it missed my skull by an inch or so and glanced off my raised shoulder instead. Then my knife connected, but my luck was bad and I hit a belt buckle. I was once told that all British gentlemen wear suspenders—excuse me, braces—but apparently Mr. Walling was no gentleman. Well, I'd already begun to suspect that.

Because of the belt, I got no penetration, but the force of my lunge was enough to make him sit down hard, temporarily breathless. The sap got away from him and thumped a couple of times, rolling downstairs. At least for the moment he was out of weapons and out of wind.

I had to settle for that, since I could sense the yellow peril at my back, looking for a soft spot in which to plant that foot-long sticker. I didn't think I had time to turn. I just kicked out rearwards like a mule. My luck was improving a little. The kick connected somewhere and sent him stumbling back downstairs, but not far enough. He caught himself by the banister and came up again, catlike, his knife ready. It was three times the length of mine, and above me Walling was returning to life and groping in his clothes for some new weapon, as yet unidentified.

I was fast running out of strategy and tactics. The stairs were too narrow for any fancy work. It's only in the movies that a lone hero can stand off two trained and armed opponents indefinitely, unless he's got long legs and plenty of room to run in. I had the legs, but the space was lacking. It was beginning to look, I reflected grimly, as if Winnie might have to find herself another stalking-horse...

There was a sudden, sharp, echoing noise below. I heard the unmistakable sound of a bullet going into flesh, and the little yellow man sighed and collapsed on top of his long knife. Footsteps rushed up the stairs, and I heard the reassuring voice of Les Crowe-Barham—I guess I knew him well enough to call him Les despite his title. I'd saved his life once and now he'd saved mine.

I glanced toward Walling, above me. Something glittered in his hand as he hesitated; then he threw it aside and fled upwards. I started after him instinctively, but there was no real point in being heroic with a four-inch knife when there was a gun handy, and I threw myself down and sideways to clear the line of fire for Crowe-Barham. Briefly, the stairway was full of sound once more, and I heard the bullets go past. They sounded unpleasantly close. Any bullet you can hear sounds unpleasantly close.

Walling made it to the third-floor landing unhit. Les came charging past me, still wearing his chauffeur's cap, taking the stairs two at a time. I sat up, and saw the weapon Walling had thrown aside: a small hypodermic syringe. It wasn't exactly what I'd expected. I started to reach for it, but Les was calling me from above, and I let the hypo go and scrambled up there. The door marked ORIENTAL EXPORTS was open. I went through it, and through the outer office, and found Les, just beyond the next door, bending over a body face down on the floor. He turned it over and looked up at me. I shook my head.

"Wrong man," I said. "Besides, even if you'd hit the guy on the stairs, which you didn't, this one's been dead for hours."

Les drew a long breath and walked deliberately to the rear of the office and opened a door, revealing a small hallway and another door leading to a kind of fire escape or outside stairway, which in turn led down into a courtyard. There was no fugitive in sight. Les put his gun away in his hip pocket. Well, every man to his own taste. I've never believed in sitting on my armaments, but techniques do vary.

We returned to the body on the floor. It was that of a middle-aged man of medium height with stiff sandy hair and a narrow little moustache. The back of the head had been smashed in, perhaps by the blackjack I'd already encountered. The fingers of the right hand were pretty badly mangled. A pair of bloody pliers lay nearby, not the most original of torture implements, but reasonably effective. I wondered if the dead man had talked, and if so, what he had had to talk about.

"Anybody you know?" I asked Les.

"Permit me to introduce you, old fellow. Mr. Matthew Helm, Mr. Ernest Walling. We've been keeping an eye on him for, ah, various reasons." He glanced at me sharply as he said it.

I said only, "Some eye."

"Also an ear," Les said. He sighed. "Sometimes I think we were better off before the profession became so cluttered with electronics. Operatives tend to sit on their rear elevations and trust the machines to do the work, instead of using their legs and brains. But my present chief is a great believer in modern equipment." He shrugged. "Walling was heard to go out for lunch. He was heard to reenter his office on the floor above. At least our fellow assumed it was Walling. Obviously he was wrong."

"Sure. They grabbed him as he came up the stairs, got as much information out of him as they needed, and another man took his place to greet me. Who was the impostor?" Les didn't answer. I glanced at him and said, "In case you didn't get a good look at the guy over your sights, he was about five-nine, about one-fifty, I'd say in his middle forties. Sandy hair and moustache like our friend here, but that's subject to change, of course. His most distinctive feature was the eyes: gray and kind of slaty-looking. He was very good, whoever he was. A little on the cautious side—he wasn't much use in the hassle, and he lit right out when the shooting started—but as an actor he was very good indeed. He lectured me on genealogy as if it were the passion of his life. I bought him completely, I'll admit, until he trotted out an accomplice who was a little too sinister to be true."

Les hesitated. "Do you still claim you are in London merely for a honeymoon, old chap? Even after this attempt to kill you?"

I remembered the hypodermic on the stairs and started to say that I wasn't certain now that homicide had been intended, at least not immediately. The act that there had been a hypo loaded and ready made it look more like kidnaping. There are easier ways of killing a man than sticking him with a needle, but it's a convenient method of keeping him asleep after you've sapped him down from behind. It depended on what the thing contained, of course, but I remembered that various other agents had disappeared for a while before they had reappeared dead. But this wasn't information I was supposed to have.

I grinned at my British colleague. "And do you still insist that you called me up just to congratulate me on my marriage and offer me a car, old chap?" He looked a little embarrassed and didn't answer right away. I said, "Come on, be a pal, tell me who the guy was."

Les said rather stiffly, "If you insist that you are not officially involved, then I must insist that I can't discuss—"

"Sure, sure," I said. "It doesn't matter. A man like that will be in the files. I'll have a list of the possibilities, and what they're working on currently, as soon as I phone the description to Washington... Wait a minute." I'd been doing some heavy thinking about the impersonator. I said, "Take away the moustache and the nervous manner; give him short gray hair and about twenty pounds more weight, and what have you got? Do you remember a certain ingenious gent named Basil?"

"Basil is dead." Les didn't really mean it. He was just trying it out to hear how it sounded. He was always a little too tricky for his own good. "Basil was executed for party disloyalty about eighteen months ago, in Moscow."

I said, "Sure. Basil is supposed to have bet on the wrong political horse. He's supposed to have got himself purged or liquidated or whatever the current euphemism may be. That's what it says on the official record—and how many officially dead men have you seen come back to life? I don't ever cross them off unless I get to bury them myself, and then I want to dig them up every couple of years to make sure they're still there. Basil, eh?"

Les sighed. "Very well. From your description, it probably was Basil. He's certainly involved. You have a good memory, old chap."

"It may be good but it's too damn slow. I wasn't expecting to walk in on a masquerade, but I really should have spotted him. Of course, I've never met him before, but I've studied his dossier plenty of times. Were his supposed disgrace and death just a cover-up for something tricky? I mean, is he still doing business for the same old firm, or did he actually get into trouble, escape execution somehow, and take employment elsewhere?" I waited, got no answer, and glanced at Les irritably. "Oh, for God's sake, man, give your security a rest!"

He said reluctantly, "We have reason to believe that Basil has changed allegiance, but we do not know who his new employers are. Now you'd better stop trying to get something for nothing, old boy, and leave quickly, unless you want to spend several hours in a police station. I will take care of the official explanations. Use the back stairs.

Sorry not to be able to drive you back to the hotel, but you can catch the underground just beyond the square."

"Sure," I said. I went to the door, remembered my manners, and looked back. "Oh, incidentally," I said, "thanks. They had me boxed. I never heard a Browning sound prettier."

His long horse face looked embarrassed. He said, "Be careful leaving, old boy. Basil may still be hanging around."

After battling treacherous impersonators and mysterious Asiatics, riding the subway seemed anticlimactic. So did my visit to a quiet library where I checked out the *Scots Peerage* reference Basil had given me, in his character of Walling. I found it quite genuine. I also, with the help of the librarian, checked on Clan McRue and learned that it was, as I'd been told, supposed to have died out—or been killed off—over two hundred years ago. I wondered if Basil was regretting having given me this much information. Apparently he'd played the Walling part straight, that being the easiest way. After all, I wasn't supposed to be going anywhere with what I'd learned.

There was no suggestion in the reference works that any member of Clan McRue had ever migrated to America and started a new line under a different version of the family name, but it was the sort of negative proposition that would be hard to establish at all, let alone in an hour. Even so, I kept the helpful librarian well after his official closing time.

When I got back to the hotel, everything looked so peaceful and respectable that I found it hard to remember that not long ago I'd been fighting for my life—or at least, if the evidence of the hypo was to be accepted, my liberty. Then I saw Vadya having a drink alone in the big formal lounge off the lobby, and the place seemed less restful. Her legs were gracefully crossed, displaying a lot of sheer nylon. I had a hunch it was an invitation, but I passed it up and started for the stairs. A polite male voice called me back.

"Your key, sir."

I turned and took the room key from the clerk behind the desk. I looked at the key with its heavy tag, which was supposed to keep you from forgetfully running off with it. The last time I'd seen it—assuming it was the same key, and I thought it was—it had been lying on the dresser upstairs beside Winnie's cigarettes, when I'd picked them up to give them to her. The man behind the desk cleared his throat discreetly.

"Madame left a note for you, sir," he said. "She asked me to be sure to give it to you when you returned."

He held out a sealed envelope of hotel stationery. I took it. My name was written on it in a funny, sloppy scrawl I'd seen before. Specimens of handwriting are, of course, part of every agent's file, and I'd studied up on Winnie's before leaving Washington.

I said slowly, "Madame went out?"

She wasn't supposed to go out. I'd asked her not to. And she was a trained operative, not a flighty kid. Having said she'd stay, she'd stay—unless she couldn't help herself.

The clerk corrected me. "Madame checked out, sir."

His face betrayed a struggle between diplomacy and curiosity. There's something about newlyweds and their problems that intrigues even hardened hotel men who've seen them come and go by the thousands.

"What do you mean, checked out?" I demanded. "You mean she took her luggage and—" I stopped abruptly, as if startling possibilities had suddenly occurred to me, which wasn't far wrong. "Did she leave alone?" I asked.

"No, a lady and a gentleman called for her, sir."

"What did they look like?"

The man hesitated. "The lady was, er, Oriental, sir."

The damn case seemed to be lousy with Fu Manchus, both male and female, or somebody was trying hard to give that impression. I wasn't really sold on the idea, not yet anyway; nor was I taking Basil's official disgrace at face value, no matter what my British colleagues might think about it. Basil had been on the same team as Vadya once, and while it isn't safe to take for granted that all Communists are going to be forever buddies, neither can you safely assume that they hate each other just because they say so.

I muttered a word of thanks to the clerk and swung away and plunged toward the stairs like a deeply troubled and preoccupied man. Under the circumstances, it didn't require a great deal of acting talent. I didn't glance toward the smart, slightly overweight lady sipping a martini in the lounge, seemingly without a care in the world. If she was waiting there for me, as seemed likely, she could wait a little longer.

7

There was nothing in the room, of course. I mean, there were no signs of violence. There were no clues, or if there were I didn't spot them as such—I'm not much of a clueman. There were no cute little last-minute oh-help-me messages scrawled in lipstick on the bathroom mirror. Well, there wouldn't be. We weren't dealing with amateurs.

That was the catch. The only amateur involved, by decree, was Winnie herself. I realized belatedly that I might as well have skipped the precaution of making her stay in the hotel. She was no safer there than elsewhere, with the instructions she carried. She was my sweet, harmless, gutless little bride, and she was under orders to remain so no matter what happened, to me or to her, until she got herself next to a gent named McRow or got herself killed. The latter possibility was one we hadn't considered as fully as we might have, since I was the one who was supposed to be running the big risks. On the other hand, I was allowed to fight back. Winnie wasn't.

If strangers called from downstairs, perhaps claiming to be old friends of mine, she had to invite them up politely. When they knocked on the door, she had to open unsuspectingly, just like the innocent honeymoon kid she was supposed to be. If she was grabbed, she had to forget everything she'd ever learned about defending herself. And if, with a couple of preliminary slaps for emphasis, she was ordered to write something at the point of a gun, she had to write, with convincing big tears of pain and fright trickling down her cheeks.

I didn't look around too hard. I didn't even want to know if they'd planted a few hearing aids on me while they were in here. It seemed unlikely they'd pass up the chance. I just sat down on the bed and tore open the envelope. The note inside was very good. Without going into details, it hinted at all kinds of fascinating secrets and relationships.

Dear Matt:

I have just learned something that hurts me very much. I'm sure you know what I mean. I've been a blind little fool. Please don't try to find me.

Winnie

I frowned at this thoughtfully. It was really a very fine note. It said all the right things to everybody who might read it, from me to the hotel maid who might find it in the wastebasket later.

To me, of course, it was a warning in double-talk. It said quite clearly that if I tried to find Winnie, she'd be hurt very much. Presumably I was supposed to wait for contact to be made, meanwhile playing the part of the older husband whose young wife had learned his dreadful secret and left him. I was supposed to keep things quiet with this story, disturbing neither the hotel management nor the authorities. The implication, not necessarily reliable, was that if I did all this, Winnie would be okay and might even be released eventually, perhaps in return for further cooperation on my part.

I stared at the note grimly. *I'm sure you know*, it said, presumably meaning that I surely knew with whom I was dealing, but I didn't really. I only knew that Vadya had moved into the hotel here at just about the same time that Basil was getting ready to receive me at Wilmot Square, but I couldn't be absolutely certain they were working together. These could have been independent actions triggered by my phone call to Walling. The first thing I had to do was determine, maybe by a process of elimination, just who did have Winnie. Of course, I'd been warned not to try to find her, but that was routine. As a desperate husband who was also a trained and ruthless agent, I wouldn't really be expected to do nothing at all.

I reached for the phone. It took me a while to learn Les's current office number, and a while longer to reach him. Then I had him on the line.

"Crowe-Barham here."

"Helm," I said. "Did you get everything taken care of at that place, *amigo*?"

"I did," he said, "but there is a feeling in the higher echelons that a certain amount of reciprocity would be very nice, old chap. If you ask for our assistance, it has been suggested, you might at least take us into your confidence."

"Who asked?" I said. "Check your tapes of the conversation, old pal. I asked nothing. You called and made the offer, unsolicited. Not that I'm not grateful, and all that jazz." Before he could speak, I went on quickly, "But I'm asking now. Are Her Majesty's troops still at my disposal? My wife is missing."

There was a brief silence; then he said quietly, "I say, I am sorry to hear it. What can we do to help?"

"I need a quiet room. A very quiet room—soundproof perhaps and a car with a deaf-and-dumb chauffeur." After a moment I added without expression, "The car and driver you lent me this afternoon would do fine."

There was another little pause. "Are you planning to leave anything in the quiet room, old boy? I mean, who cleans up afterwards, you or we?" I didn't say anything. There was yet another silence. I could visualize him frowning, perhaps chewing or tugging at his moustache, while he made up his mind. Then his voice came again: "Ah, well, accidents sometimes happen in this work, don't you know? If one should occur, just leave the debris, slip the latch, and let the door lock behind you. We'll take care of things again. Incidentally, it would seem as if somebody wanted you both alive. We found a hypodermic on the stairs at Wilmot Square. The contents would have put you under for quite a while, but they would not have killed you."

"I see. Thanks for the information."

"There have been some very odd kidnappings lately. We do not quite understand the purpose. Killing, yes, but not kidnaping. Perhaps you have something to contribute on the subject."

"I'm afraid not," I said. "All I know is that my wife is missing."

"To be sure." His voice was cool. "Well, where and when will you want the car?"

I told him. Afterwards, I replaced the phone, got up and made a face at my image in the dresser mirror. I don't really like asking help from people I have to lie to, or lying to people I have to ask for help. I got my suitcase, threw it on the bed and did some tricks to open a camouflaged compartment holding, among other ingenious toys, my little .38 Special revolver: the snub-nosed, five-shot, aluminum-framed model that, too light to absorb much of the recoil of its heavy cartridge, will damn near tear your hand off when you fire it, not to mention blasting holes in both eardrums.

It is, in my opinion, just about as logical a weapon for a man in a supposedly hush-hush job as a 20mm antitank gun, but it's what the efficiency experts in Washington have decided we need. Regulations state that we must keep the miniature cannon handy at all times, cover permitting, but no experienced operative takes that rule seriously. I'll carry it in my suitcase because I have to, but I'm damned if I'll wear it unnecessarily. Nothing can get you into more trouble, particularly in a foreign country, than a firearm. Winnie, of course, had orders to carry no weapons whatever on this assignment, in line with her innocent act. When the time came for her to do her stuff, I was supposed to supply whatever she needed out of my private stock.

I closed the secret compartment, tucked the wicked little gun under my waistband, buttoned my coat and topcoat over it, and put my hat back on. There was one more item I required, and it was one that wasn't supplied in the standard agent's travel kit. I didn't have anything suitable in my belongings. My only belt was needed to keep my pants up. I might even need it for other purposes, sooner or later, since it's a rather special belt.

Luck came to my rescue—if it was luck. Maybe I'd found a clue after all. In hastily cleaning out the dresser, packing under duress, Winnie had apparently overlooked one small drawer. It contained some gloves, some nylons still in the plastic factory package, some odds and ends of cosmetics and costume jewelry, and a couple of belts. I chose a wide, black, soft-leather number with a big, tricky, dramatic buckle. Flashy though it was, it looked as if it might possibly be strong enough for what I had in mind. I coiled it up and dropped it into my pocket and went downstairs.

Claridge's lounge bore no resemblance to the kind of dark, cramped chrome-plated cocktail-trap you'd find in, say, a New York hotel. It was a high-ceilinged, light, rambling, luxurious, pillared room that could have been the anteroom of a castle or palace where high-class people awaited audience with royalty. Silent waiters glided about with drinks procured from some unknown source. Nothing so vulgar as a bar was in evidence.

Vadya, still sitting at the same table near the door, was doing her part to maintain the tone of the place. She looked very high-class indeed. I walked up and seated myself facing her after tossing my hat and coat on an empty chair. I ordered a martini from the waiter who materialized at my side.

Vadya showed no surprise at seeing me. "Better make it a double, darling," she said lazily. "They serve them in thimbles around here."

"Make it a double," I said.

"And get me another, please."

"And another for the lady," I said.

The waiter bowed and vanished. I leaned back and regarded Vadya with critical interest. After all, aside from our momentary encounter in the hotel doorway, it had been a couple of years since I'd seen her last.

She was putting on quite a show. Her hairdo was big but elaborately simple, if the words aren't incompatible. The thrown-back mink stole was the real stuff. Her suit was tan wool—beige is the technical term, I believe—with a straight, short, close-fitting skirt, and a straight, short, loose-fitting jacket. I wondered idly what had happened to the old-fashioned notion of cutting jackets to fit the female human form. I'd thought it was kind of a nice idea, but then, fashion-wise, I'm obviously way behind the times.

There was a high-collared blouse of the kind of silk associated with caterpillars and mulberry trees instead of chemical vats. Her nylons were so sheer as to be almost nonexistent, just a nebulous hint of stocking, and her pumps had heels a yard long and an eighth of an inch in diameter. Well, almost. She looked sleek and well-fed and expensive.

The last time I'd seen her, on the other side of the Atlantic, she'd been playing a younger, leaner, and cheaper role. I could remember her dressed in grubby white shorts, as short and tight as the law allowed, and a limp boy's shirt with a missing button. I could also recall her dressed in even less. It had been quite an intriguing assignment, the one that had brought us together out there in the great Southwest.

Fortunately, our national interests had run more or less parallel—it happens occasionally—but we'd played a fast game of trickery and double-cross before this became apparent. I'd put her on a plane afterwards and shipped her out of the country instead of wringing her neck on general principles, as I undoubtedly should have. Winnie, the hard-boiled little kook, would have called that sentimentality, I suppose. Softhearted Helm, the Galahad of the undercover services. Well, hell, you can't kill everybody.

I said, "If that's all you, doll, you've been eating too much. I don't like my women pudgy."

"Your women!" she murmured.

I grinned. "Well, I seem to recall staking a claim of sorts, the way it's usually done. In a motel in Tucson, if I remember correctly."

"But now you have a pretty little blonde wife, I am told. And you are celebrating your honeymoon." She was watching me closely. She waited a little, perhaps giving me a chance to go into my bereaved-husband act, but I knew her well enough to know that my only chance of making her believe I was really married was not to work at it at all. I had to play it cool and straight. Waving my arms and tearing my hair would get me nowhere; she'd know at once I was faking. When I didn't react, she sighed theatrically. "Ah, to forget me so soon, for another woman, darling! I am hurt."

The waiter was putting our drinks on the table. When he had gone, I said, "The only way you'll ever be hurt, Vadya, is with an axe. What are you doing here, anyway?"

"Isn't it obvious? I heard you were here, so I came flying to see you."

"Sure," I said. "I am flattered."

She let her playful smile fade, and said, "Strangely enough, I am telling you the truth, Matthew."

I let that pass. "How am I supposed to introduce you, if anyone should ask?"

She said, in an accented voice, "Ah, you may call me Madame Dumaire, *chéri*. Madame Evelyn Dumaire. Monsieur Dumaire, unfortunately, is no longer among the living, but fortunately he left his widow well provided for."

"I can see that," I said, with a glance at the expensive furs. "Okay, Evelyn. And God help the French. I hope they have the 'Mona Lisa' nailed down tight or it will be in Moscow by morning."

She shook her head. "No. It wasn't the 'Mona Lisa,' of course—who would waste a good agent's time on that smirking canvas female?—and I have been taken off the Paris assignment, anyway. They called me at lunch. They said, 'There is a man in London with whom you are acquainted, Vadya. He spared your life once, the record shows. This would seem to indicate that you are the best person we have to negotiate with him. There is no time to construct a new cover. You will go over there—immediately, by jet airplane—as plump Madame Dumaire.'" She smiled. "You see, I am being devastatingly frank. I am letting you know from the start that I was sent here because you were here. Because my employers think I am conscienceless enough to try to capitalize on our old friendship. As of course I am."

It wasn't exactly what I'd expected. To give myself time to think about it, I said, "Some friendship! I've still got the scars where you and your partner played tic-tac-toe on my chest with a hot soldering iron."

She said, quite undisturbed, "It was a misunderstanding. Poor Max."

"Poor Max, hell," I said. "After that little branding session, what made him think I wouldn't shoot when he tried to pull a gun on me next day? Well, I guess you could call that a misunderstanding, too." I grimaced. "Are you serious? Do you really expect me to believe you were sent here officially to renew our old acquaintance?"

She said, "Don't be so clever and suspicious, my friend. Remember that sometimes the direct approach is the best. Anyway, it is the one I have been instructed to use. You see, we know why you are here in England."

I said, poker-faced, "And why am I here?"

"You are here because there is a crazy man at large, an American scientist named McRow. This man is working on a fantastic biological weapon with which he apparently intends to blackmail the world, my country included. At least that is the intelligence we have received. Well, there are many crazy men with big ideas about getting rich, and this one would not worry us, were it not for the fact that he has acquired strong backing somewhere. McRow's motives seem to be simple and financial, but we are not sure of the motives of his backers. They could be military, and there are certain countries eastward that, while they boast of their ancient civilizations, are not, we feel, advanced enough politically to be trusted with a weapon such as this."

"You mean they don't have quite the right Communist slant on things?"

"Don't be sarcastic, Matthew. They don't have quite the right democratic slant on things, either. There is also a certain racial factor. I do not believe many would weep, out there in the East, if all white men were to get very sick and die. There are even some irresponsible leaders out there, we feel, who would willingly sacrifice large

parts of their own populations to achieve this purpose—
as long as a loyal elite was assured of survival. That could
be achieved by a serum or vaccine; and we think that is
what McRow is now working to perfect, since he has
already shown that he can produce super-virulent forms
of several common diseases. He will presumably select
the one for which he can most easily produce an effective
antidote." She drew a long breath. "You see, I am being
absolutely frank; I am describing the problem to you
exactly as it was described to me. Naturally, we would
like this development for our own, but although they have
tried hard, our people have failed to get it. So have yours."

"What makes you think so?"

"The fact that you are here makes us think so, for
one thing," said Vadya. She laughed softly. "We are
specialists, darling, you and I. We are not called upon to
capture men alive, or bring home their nasty little secrets.
When we are summoned everyone knows what it means.
It means that all other methods have failed, and time is
getting short, and there is only one thing left to do." She
looked at me earnestly across the table. "I am instructed
to cooperate with you in any reasonable way, Matthew,
until this international threat is removed. Until this man
is killed and his laboratory destroyed."

There was a little silence. Presently I said in a tentative
way, "You know, the funny thing is, I really am on my
honeymoon." She didn't say anything to this, and after a
moment I went on: "Of course, that doesn't mean I'm out
of the business entirely."

She smiled faintly. "I thought not."

"I'll have to know a little more before I get in touch with Washington. Suppose we have dinner together and you tell me exactly what you have in mind."

"Yes, of course. Do you want to eat here?"

I threw a look toward the impressively formal dining room opening off the lounge, and said, "These Claridge waiters give a poor country boy from New Mexico a raging inferiority complex. I seem to remember a little place off Piccadilly Circus where we can relax and talk."

"Whatever you say."

She drew her furs around her, and waited for me to rise and attend to her chair like a gentleman. Then she pulled on her gloves, picked up her purse, and smiled at me over her shoulder to indicate that she was ready.

We walked out of the lounge together, and through the lobby to the street. Les was right on the ball. The doorman didn't even have time to offer his services before the gleaming silvery sedan was gliding to the curb in front of the hotel. Vadya stopped and glanced at me with sudden suspicion.

"So I've got friends in London," I said. "Hop in."

She frowned at the chauffeur-driven Rolls, and looked back at me. "It is not that I do not trust you, darling, but I think I would prefer a taxicab."

"Sure," I said, close behind her. "But get in anyway. If I have to shoot from this angle, we'll get blood and guts all over that lovely vehicle, and that would be a pity, wouldn't it?"

8

Riding away from there, nobody spoke for a little. Vadya shifted position beside me, and reached up as if to rearrange her furs. I brought the snub-nosed revolver out where she could see it.

"Hands off the pelts," I said. "I once knew a girl—a colleague of yours, as a matter of fact—who had a real tricky fur that looked just like that. She's dead now, poor kid."

Vadya let her gloved hands sink back into her lap. "You're making a mistake, Matthew," she said quietly.

She might well be right; but I couldn't afford to show any doubts. "It happens to us all," I said. "You make one, I make one. You wouldn't want me to be perfect and show you up."

"I don't know what you mean—"

Our aristocratic chauffeur spoke without turning his head. "There's a Mini following us, sir."

It took me a moment to remember that this was the

British way of referring affectionately to those boxy little Morrisses and Austins—they're identical except for the nameplate—that have the engine mounted crosswise to operate a tricky frontwheel drive, and tires borrowed from a small motorscooter. I didn't look back. Instead I looked at Vadya. Her face was expressionless. Well, it would be.

I said, "That's okay, driver. Let's keep him on ice. The more the merrier. If I don't get the information I want out of the woman, I'll just work on down the line. You can keep him from interfering, can't you?"

"Yes, sir."

Vadya stirred uneasily beside me. "Matthew—"

I said, "Not now. You'll get your chance to talk, later."

We finished the drive without further conversation. The car stopped in a rather shabby, dark street of row houses several stories high. I had no real idea where we were. London is a big city and few foreigners learn it all. Les came around to open the door. I backed out cautiously, keeping Vadya covered as she emerged in her turn.

"It is the first door on the right on the first floor, sir," Les said. "Ah, I believe you Americans call that the second floor, sir. One flight up, sir."

"Very good."

"I will be waiting, sir. There will be no interference."

"Thanks. Come on, Mrs. Dumaire."

Vadya started to speak and thought better of it. She started to yank her furs straight, but saw my gun steady, and thought better of that, too. She turned sharply and marched into the house ahead of me. The downstairs doors were unlocked. There was dim but adequate light in the dusty stairway, which looked somewhat like another London stairway I had reason to remember. The woman ahead of me turned right at the top, and stopped at the proper door.

"Open it," I said.

Unlike most hall doors, it opened outward. It had to, since there was another door right behind it, opening the other way. I saw Vadya take stock of this soundproof arrangement. She glanced at me, shrugged, pushed the second door open, and went into the room beyond. I followed her, closing both doors behind us, locking the inner one, and pocketing the key.

Aside from the double door, it seemed like a room that matched the run-down neighborhood. It had a threadbare rug, a battered dresser, a tired old bed, and a single heavy armchair that seemed in better repair than the rest of the furnishings. There was an enameled tin basin, and a water pitcher, on the dresser. The cracked handle of a china thunder mug peeked out from under the bed. The illumination came from an ancient fixture suspended from the ceiling that had once burned gas. It gave surprisingly good light considering its apparent age.

Vadya had turned to face me. Her glamorous hairdo and glossy furs looked completely out of place in the dismal room. I felt a momentary qualm, but what the hell, she wasn't really the pretty, plump, fashionable Madame Dumaire. She was just a cheap hired actress masquerading in a fancy-dress outfit paid for, no doubt, with state funds.

She said, "Matthew, really, I—"

The nice white kid gloves were a handicap, from her point of view. They not only made her fingers a little less nimble than they might have been, they made it very easy for me to see what her hands were doing. When one disappeared inside the furs, I socked her hard, right in the middle of her expensive suit. She doubled up, gasping. I clipped her judiciously across the neck and she fell to the floor. I mean, you can ask questions all night and get nowhere and prove nothing. If you're going the interrogation route anyway, you might as well save everybody a lot of time by showing right at the start that you don't mind bruising your knuckles.

I picked up the purse she had dropped, and yanked her furs free. She was already beginning to stir. Waiting for her to recover, I looked the stuff over. There was nothing in the purse beyond the usual feminine accessories and some official items confirming her identity as the widowed, wealthy Madame Evelyn Dumaire, citizeness of France. I tossed it on the bed.

The furs, as I'd expected, proved more rewarding. A cunningly hidden pocket at one end yielded up a tiny automatic pistol. Another secret fold in the satin lining produced a slim little plastic case. Inside was an interesting assortment of pills and powders and the means with which to administer them. It was the other side's counterpart of our special drug kit, a sample of which reposed in my suitcase at the hotel.

I remembered that, down in Mexico, Vadya had been

a fast girl with a Mickey. At that time she'd happened to be working to our mutual advantage, but it was something to keep in mind. I tossed the things on the bed, and went over and nudged her with my toe.

"Wake up," I said. "But do it slowly." She didn't move.

I said, "Cut it out, Vadya. Don't play possum with me. This is your old friend Matt speaking. Remember Matt, the guy you once carved your initials on with a hot iron? Get up and get into that chair, and be very, very careful doing it."

After a moment she moved, and pushed herself to a crouching position, and looked up at me through the hair that had fallen into her eyes. She started to speak, changed her mind, rose, and walked unsteadily to the big chair and sat down. I went to stand over her.

"I've got your gun," I said. "I've got your cute little portable pharmacy. There's one more thing I'm going to have from you before we commence the singing lesson. Will you give it to me now, or do I have to strip you to find it?"

"I... I don't understand."

I said, "Cut it out, Vadya. Save it for the peasants. We're both pros here. You've got one somewhere. Hand it over. The kill-me capsule."

Her eyes narrowed slightly, perhaps with a hint of apprehension. My taking the trouble, before questioning her, to separate her from the death-pill most agents carry made it seem as if I really meant business. Well, it was supposed to.

After a moment she drew a long breath and pulled off her left-hand glove and tossed it to me. I caught it. "The button," she said.

I examined the glove and found she'd told the truth. The small wrist button wasn't a button at all. While I was looking at it, she stripped off the second glove and tossed it toward the bed, and at last made the customary feminine motions of patting her hair into place, pulling down her skirt, and making a rueful face at a nylon torn at the knee.

"You play very rough, darling," she said. "Look at my poor stocking."

I said, "To hell with your poor stocking. It's your working costume, isn't it? Like a blacksmith's apron or a mechanic's coverall. You expect it to take a beating; don't give me that poor-stocking bit. You'll put three pairs on the expense account when you turn in your report, if you live so long. Get your mind off your nylons and start worrying about your neck, doll. They can't buy you a new one of those."

She laughed in my face. "Are you really trying to frighten me, Matthew? Do you know me so little then?" I didn't say anything. I just waited for the question she had to ask, unless she was going to admit she knew why we were here, and it came: "Why have you brought me here? What do you want?"

I looked at her sitting there, a little mussed and rumpled now, no longer quite in character, with her phony accent, her phony identity, and her voluptuous, phony figure. I thought of a smaller, browner, blonder girl whose life could very well depend on what happened here in the next few minutes. I reached into my pocket and took out the black leather belt.

"I want," I said, "the answer to just one question. I want to know where Winnie is."

She looked quickly at the belt. Again there was a hint of apprehension in her eyes. "Winnie? Who is Winnie?"

It was the first real break. I knew a great sense of relief; I wasn't making a mistake after all. I wasn't bullying an innocent woman—well, innocent in one respect, at least. Because even if Vadya wasn't remotely involved in the kidnaping, she'd know who Winnie was. Hell, she'd given me a description while we were talking at Claridge's. She'd said: *and now you have a pretty little blonde wife, I'm told.* She was bound to have been told the name, also, as part of her briefing.

Her instinctive pretense of ignorance was the kind of nervous reflex that betrays you when you've been waiting hours to put on a dumb act and had a few drinks, and taken a few blows in the process. If the name had had no guilty associations for her, she wouldn't have been so quick to deny knowing it.

She realized it, and said, "Oh, I remember now. That is your new little wife? She is missing?"

I said, "Not very good, Vadya. Not good at all."

"You think I know something about it? But I assure you—"

"Cut it out," I said. "Never mind the denials,

sweetheart. We'll just take them as said. You don't know anything, you never did know anything, you never will know anything. Okay? That's what you were going to tell me, isn't it?"

"Matthew, I—"

I said, "We both know how these question-and-answer sessions go, so let's see if we can't dispense with some of the usual corn. Here is a belt." I held it up. "It will be around your neck—I wasn't kidding when I said you should be worrying about your neck. The tongue will be through the buckle here, so. I'll be behind your chair. I'll ask my question, for the record this time. I'll give you a reasonable time to answer. If you refuse, or start telling me a lot of junk about what you don't know and didn't do, I'll pull on this end here and cut you off. Then I'll loosen it again and give you another chance. Maybe I'll even give you a third chance. It depends on my patience and on whether I sense, shall we say, a growing spirit of cooperation. But make no mistake, before we leave this room, I'll know where my wife is, or you'll be dead."

I stopped. It was very quiet in the room. The soundproofing apparently extended to the windows facing the street. Not a murmur of traffic reached us from the great city outside. Vadya looked at the black leather noose, and licked her lips.

"Why… why, you are serious, Matt. You are really threatening to torture and kill me—"

"Good," I said. "That's much better. You're really catching on. I knew the idea would penetrate eventually.

However, I'm not going to torture you, not in the ordinary sense of inflicting pain in the hope of breaking you down. I do know you, Vadya. I know you're pretty tough. I don't expect you to spill anything just because it hurts. Therefore I'm giving you a clear-cut choice. If you talk, you live. If you don't talk, you die. It's as simple as that."

"I don't know where your wife is! I didn't even know she was… missing. I don't know anything about it!"

"Sure, sure," I said. I walked around the chair and dropped the belt over her head and drew the loop up tight enough so that she was pulled against the back of the chair. "Can you breathe?" I asked.

Her voice was strained: "Yes, barely. Matthew, I swear—"

"Just one thing more," I said. "When I cut you off, you obviously won't be able to talk. Hit the arm of the chair with your hand when you're ready to give me what I want. Okay? Are you ready for the question?"

"Matt, I—"

"Here it comes," I said. "The show is now on the air, and no extraneous dialogue is permitted." I drew a long breath and leaned forward to speak in her ear. "Where is Winnie?"

"Matt, you're making a terrible mist—"

I took a strain on the belt. Vadya's voice was cut off abruptly. She started to try to pull the noose free; then she remembered and beat one hand quickly against the chair arm. I slacked off. I heard her breathe deeply and raggedly.

"I told you," I said. "I warned you. Don't give me any

of that innocent crap, Vadya. Here we go again. Where is Winnie?"

"Darling, how can I possibly tell you what I don't know—"

The noose cut her short. She started beating at the chair immediately, but I gave her several seconds before I eased off and let her breathe.

"I'm getting tired, doll," I said. "Third time coming up. It could be the last one. I can't spend all night on you."

"Matt," she cried. "Matt, you must believe me. I really don't know… I haven't any idea…"

I said, "Your Moscow alma mater will be real proud of you, honey. Maybe they'll even put up a little posthumous plaque in the hall for other trainees to see: *In Memory of Vadya, Dumb to the Death.* Hell, I know it's the prescribed routine, but is it really worth it? Would your employers hold you to it if you could ask them? Is one lousy little blonde worth the life of a trained, experienced agent?" I put a little pressure on the strap and leaned forward. "Where is she, damn you? Where's Winnie? Where are your people holding her… No, keep your damn hands down!"

"Matt, please, I can't breathe!"

"For God's sake cut it out!" I snapped. "Can't you get it through your head that you're going to *die* if you don't come through? For the last time, where's my wife?"

"Matt," she gasped, "Matt, I swear… *Matt, don't!*"

She was pretty good, all frightened and desperate. Well, I'd been pretty good, too, all mad and menacing. We were two old pros hamming it up for each other, but I was the guy holding the end of the noose.

"Goodbye, baby," I said. "When you get to hell, give my regards to your friend Max. He thought I was bluffing, too."

She grabbed for the belt with both hands as I yanked it up tight. She was too late to get her fingers under it. She came to her feet, clawing at her throat, and lunged away from me. I felt the loop pull even tighter, and let go rather than risk breaking her neck or some essential part of it.

I came around the chair fast, expecting to have a fight on my hands. Instead, I found her on her knees, clawing desperately at the strap about her neck. The soft black belt, instead of releasing when I let it go, seemed to have locked into place as if obeying some murderous impulse of its own. Vadya's eyes were bulging and her face was darkening. She fell to the floor, rolling about convulsively, while her frantic nails ripped the collar of her blouse and drew blood from her neck but made no impression on the taut black leather.

It was going a little farther than I'd intended. I mean, no matter what threats I'd made for effect, she was no use to me dead; and while I did owe her something for the fun she'd had with a hot soldering iron a couple of years back, it wasn't really a debt that weighed heavily on my mind.

I managed, after a couple of tries, to pin her to the floor. It took all my strength to hold her down while I shoved the loosened hair forward so I could get at the noose. I tried to free it, and it wouldn't release. I looked at it more closely—as closely as her violent struggles would let me—and realized at last just what it was I had found among Winnie's gloves and hose and hankies. It was no wonder she'd "accidentally" managed to leave it behind. It wasn't something a shy young bride would normally carry in her trousseau. It could have betrayed her, if her captors had got a good look at it.

Apparently I wasn't the only one in the organization who liked trick belts. This was a new one on me: an efficient, camouflaged garotte. The fancy buckle was actually a locking device, designed to jam solid when a certain amount of strain was put on it. Of course you could wear the thing as an ordinary, decorative belt, if you had a twenty-one-inch waist, until you needed it for other purposes. That was the idea.

Vadya's struggles were diminishing. I searched for a release catch and couldn't find one. I reached into my pocket for my knife, but realized I'd practically have to cut the girl's throat to free her, the way the strap was embedded in the flesh. While I hesitated, she stopped moving altogether. I took advantage of her stillness to make another quick study of the flashy buckle, and saw at last how it worked, and pressed the right decoration the right way. The belt came loose. I pulled it off and rolled Vadya over.

She looked very bad, but it hadn't been much over a minute, and they've been brought back from much farther away than that. I got her arms going, the way artificial respiration is done these days. It used to be you could sit on the victim comfortably and just push at the ribs, but this new method is supposed to be more effective. I haven't got a great deal of faith in it, but either it worked or she was getting ready to breathe anyway: pretty soon her chest started to heave and the ugly, congested color began to die from her face. Presently her eyes came open.

"Damn you!" she whispered. Her voice was a hoarse croak.

"Sure," I said. "Can you sit up?"

With my help, she managed to sit up against the end of the bed. She fumbled the tangled hair out of her face and felt her bruised and lacerated neck. Her hand made contact with the dangling collar of her blouse. She grasped it with vague curiosity and held it out for identification. The sight of the torn rag of silk seemed to shock her. She let it fall and looked down at herself, dismayed by what her violent struggles had done to her Madame Dumaire disguise.

"Oh, God, what a mess!" she croaked. Then she shrugged fatalistically. A funny, wry little grin came to her lips. "Ah, well, as you say it is a working costume and expendable. But you will have to lend me your coat to go home in. Help me up, darling."

I helped her up and steadied her as she swayed. I said, "Don't get your hopes up, doll. There was a little matter of an address, remember?"

I heard her breath catch. She looked at me with an expression of horror. Her blue eyes were big and dark in her pale face.

"Oh, you can't…!" she whispered hoarsely. "I… I really don't know… Matthew, you *can't*, not again!"

There was real fear in her voice—at least it sounded very real. Doubt crept back into my mind. She was good, I knew, but was she good enough to keep up the act after being choked almost to death? For a while I had been absolutely sure she had the answer, but now I felt my assurance wavering.

I said, making my voice hard, "Baby, do you remember a garage in Tucson? And a chair with a man tied in it? And a nice new electric soldering iron plugged into the wall? Somehow, I don't seem to recall anybody turning me loose just because I happened to pass out temporarily."

I picked up the belt and jerked my head. "Get back to your seat."

She hesitated, and started to move dully toward the chair; then I heard a sob and she went to her knees, clinging to the foot of the bed. She turned her head painfully to look up at me. There were real tears in her eyes.

"Shoot me!" she gasped. "I mean it! You'll kill me in the end, anyway. Well, at least do it quickly, damn you! Don't put that… that thing on me again! It won't do you any good. I don't know anything about your damn wife! We haven't got her, I swear it!"

"If you haven't, who has?"

She hesitated. She looked away. "Go ask Madame Ling."

"Madame who?"

Vadya looked up again and spoke breathlessly. "She's the one who took your little blonde away. She and one of her men. I saw them from the lounge. Ask at the desk, they'll tell you. If you'd done a little simple investigating, instead of jumping at conclusions—"

I said, "Hell, I talked to the desk man. So what? An Oriental stooge is no harder to hire than an Occidental one, in a cosmopolitan city like London, and you'd know just where to go, wouldn't you?"

"Why would I lie to you?" she demanded. "If I had your wife, would I deny it? Would I not boast of it and use it as a club against you?"

I said, "You might be that dumb. And then you might be smart enough to know you'd never get any useful cooperation out of me that way. People in our line of work don't make good blackmailees." I drew a long breath. "Well, all right. Who's this Madame Ling supposed to be, anyway?"

9

Les disapproved of me. He'd watched Vadya come out of the building with me, a bit unsteadily. She was wearing my raincoat to cover the more spectacular damage, but it couldn't conceal her wrecked hairdo and ruined nylons. It was hard to believe there was an agent around who still believed in a chivalrous double standard, but Les shot me a reproachful glance as I helped her into the Rolls and got in beside her. He was obviously regretting his part in this ungentlemanly affair.

We rode away in silence. After a while I asked, "Have we still got an escort, driver?"

"Yes, sir. They waited up the street, but they made no attempt to interfere in the lady's behalf. They are behind us now."

I glanced questioningly at Vadya. She shook her head to indicate she knew nothing about the car astern. It could even be the truth. She could be playing this as straight as she'd claimed—with a few mental reservations, of course.

As for the car behind, the purpose of this open surveillance, and the identity of the shadowers, would probably become apparent sooner or later. In the meantime, I had to let Washington know what was going on.

I said, "Driver, please let me off at a pay phone somewhere near the hotel. Then you can take the lady wherever she wants to go." When the car stopped near a phone booth, I got out and turned to look at Vadya. "If I was wrong," I said, "I'm sorry. But only a little."

She was back in control again, if she'd ever been out of it. She laughed and managed to make her hoarse voice sound quite sexy as she said, "If you come by my room in the morning, darling, I'll give you back your coat. I might even give you breakfast, to show there are no hard feelings."

"It's a date," I said.

She pulled my coat collar closer about her neck. "You can let me off at Claridge's, Sir Leslie," she said, just to let us know that our childish play-acting hadn't fooled her: she'd known who he was all along.

I stepped back and watched them drive away. The little Mini went by as I was entering the phone booth. It was a neutral tan color and there were two men in it. I didn't recognize the driver, and I couldn't see the man in the left-hand seat clearly. The throaty sound of the exhaust made me look more sharply at the car itself, realizing that it wasn't a run-of-the-mill Austin 850, but the souped-up version known as an Austin-Cooper, modified by a race-car manufacturer for British drivers who wanted to make like Stirling Moss but who couldn't afford the price of a Lotus or an Aston-Martin.

Well, it was Les's problem now. London was his town, and he could presumably take care of himself in it. If he'd wanted my advice or help, he'd have asked. I got into the booth, called our local relay man—a guy I'd never met and never expected to meet—and told him to put me through to Washington. A few minutes later I had Mac on the line. I gave him the story fast. After I'd finished, he was silent for several seconds.

"Do you believe her?" he asked at last.

"Vadya? Hell, no," I said. "That is, I don't believe I scared her nearly as badly as she pretended. I mean, that on-the-knees please-kill-me-now routine was pretty corny. On the other hand, she could be telling the truth for reasons of her own. Like she just figured we'd played enough sadistic games for one night, at her expense, and it was time to toss me a bone. Or like she'd wanted to point me in the direction of this comic-strip Dragon Lady character all along, but figured she'd first better take enough of a beating to make it look as if I'd forced the information out of her. Which still leaves the question of whether a Madame Ling really took Winnie, or Vadya just decided to frame her for the job. Do we know Madame Ling?"

"We should." Mac's voice was dry. "I do. And you would, if you'd done the required amount of work in the recognition room."

"Yes, sir," I said. "I confess my negligence, sir. I may have concentrated on the nationalities I expected to have to deal with here in Britain. Besides, I don't have a very good memory for Asiatic names or Asiatic faces, even good-looking female ones. Vadya says this one works out of Peking."

"Yes. That is another reason I assigned Claire to you. There had been some unconfirmed rumors of Chinese involvement, and I thought her experience out there might be useful to you."

"Yes, sir," I said. "In the future, I'd be flattered if you'd share your unconfirmed rumors with me, sir. The British seem to have heard the same rumor, judging by the fact that they apparently hauled Crowe-Barham in from Hong Kong to work on the case. And there's no doubt that the knife-man working with Basil was Oriental, which seems to make a link between Basil and Madame Ling. Do we have any further evidence along those lines? Is there any suggestion, for instance, that when Basil escaped that Moscow firing squad, he headed east?"

"Not that I know of. He was supposed to be dead, remember. But it's certainly a possibility, and it would explain how he managed to drop out of sight so completely for so long. I will check our Far Eastern sources."

I said, "Vadya says Ling, female, is one of Peking's top agents, a very handsome, intelligent, and nasty wench of indeterminate age, unprintable character, and no scruples at all. That's just one woman's opinion of another, of course. The point is that Madame Ling seems to be fairly high-echelon material, maybe high enough to be given this whole McRow show to run, with Basil hired as a kind of field assistant. And if we make the wild assumption that Vadya was telling the truth for once in her life, these are the people who have Winnie."

Mac said, "Let us hope so. With a little luck, that could work out very well. At least it would put one of you in the enemy camp, so to speak."

Sometimes he seems a bit cold-blooded even for this business. "Sure, it's great, sir," I said sourly. "Always assuming, of course, that Winnie's still alive and doesn't wind up full of super-streptococci or something before I can find her and give her a hand. I haven't got a lead worth mentioning unless..." I stopped, frowning.

"Unless what, Eric?"

"Unless they're still interested in grabbing me, too. If so, their obvious move is to use Winnie as bait, particularly if they're inclined to believe our marriage is genuine. The note they left hints at some such intention. I mean, it warns me not to try to find her. Now, they know damn well I'm going to try to find her—unless I have some hope of making a deal for her. I think that's what they're hinting at here. What they're saying is, in effect: don't call us, we'll call you."

"Maybe, but you could be reading too much into that note, Eric. And even if you aren't, it could be merely a way of trying to keep you quiet while they get far away with Claire. But if they should get in touch with you, what do you propose to do?"

I said, "Why, in that case, sir, my anxiety for my bride will of course be so great that I will eagerly obey any instructions given me, forgetting the most elementary precautions. I'll be caught with my pants down. It will be most humiliating, for an operative of my age and experience. That will put two of us in the enemy camp. Between us, we ought to get the job done somehow."

He hesitated briefly. "It's a risky plan, with both of you in their hands. And it depends entirely on their making contact with you. We can't wait too long for that. There are indications that Dr. McRow considers his work almost finished. Various friendly governments have reported feelers from underground sources. There have been hints of demands soon to be made—financial demands—coupled with veiled threats."

"We've got it from the other side of the fence, too, sir," I said. "Vadya intimated that her government was expecting some kind of international blackmail. Do we have any idea of just what we're all being threatened with?"

"The Black Death has now apparently been mentioned officially. You will recall that's what killed Buchanan, in a super-virulent form. In the fourteenth century, I am told, the old-fashioned brand wiped out twenty-five per cent of the population of Europe in a relatively short time."

"Well, I guess we've still got enough rats and fleas to pass the new version around, if somebody gets it started," I said.

"Precisely," Mac said. "Which brings us to Vadya's suggestion that our two nations cooperate for the good of humanity. Do you think there is any possibility that she could be sincere?"

"Vadya could never be sincere, she doesn't know how,"

I said. "But I think she means it up to a point, sir. I think her people are just as much in the dark as we are, but they'd like to know for sure how much that is, hence the frank and earnest approach. Anything they learn from us, under the circumstances, is gravy. Naturally, the minute Vadya and I, working together, turn up a good lead, she'll put a knife in my back, a bullet in my head, or a Mickey in my drink, and proceed, alone, to carry out her instructions concerning McRow, whatever they really are. Assuming I'm silly enough to let her."

"Precisely," Mac said. "Well, with that understanding, if she's still willing after tonight's experience at your hands, you have permission to make whatever deals with her you see fit, and keep them or not as you see fit."

I said, "She'll be willing. She's a pro, sir. She's not going to hold a little strangulation against me, any more than I hold a little toasting against her. She's already invited me to breakfast in her room."

"Very well. Of course you will keep in mind that the lady does not have to survive after she ceases to be useful to us. As for Madame Ling, and also Basil, I'll try to have some more information when you call in next."

"Yes, sir," I said. "Of course, that could be quite a while, if somebody does get in touch with me about my vanished bride. Well, I'd better get back to the hotel and start chewing my fingernails in public."

"Don't wait too long for a contact. If you haven't been approached by, say, noon tomorrow, you had better leave the inside angles to Claire, and head for Scotland and see if you can't turn up something around Ullapool. If they don't intend using her to trap you, we can hope they'll transport her up there. Dr. McRow seems to frown on the ordinary methods of homicide. He apparently prefers to have his enemies taken alive, so he can use them for experimental purposes."

I said, "I'm sure that makes Winnie feel real great, wherever she is."

I walked back to Claridge's. It was raining a little, the pavements were wet and shiny, and everybody was still driving on the wrong side of the street. You get used to it eventually, but I hadn't yet. I was pretty certain that nobody followed me, which was a little discouraging. I would have preferred some sign of active interest. Well, maybe they figured they knew where to find me when they wanted me.

Reaching the hotel, I climbed the stairs and let myself into the room. I must have had some kind of foolish hope that Winnie might have returned in my absence, because it was a disappointment to find the place as empty as when I'd left it. I tossed my hat on a chair, tossed the black belt back in the drawer where I'd found it, and was about to head back downstairs to drown my sorrows where people could see me, when the phone began to ring. I grabbed it quickly.

"Mr. Helm?"

"This is Mr. Helm," I said.

"There is a lady here to see you, sir," said the voice of the switchboard girl. "She is waiting in the lounge. A

Miss Glenmore, from America."

It took me a while to remember where I'd heard the name, even though it was, in a sense, my own.

10

I spotted her by the tartan. I mean, I hadn't stopped at the desk for a guide to lead me to her, wanting to look her over unseen, if possible, before she saw me, but there were quite a few people in the lounge to complicate the identification. But I knew the slim, brown-haired girl sitting alone near the piano was the one I wanted when I saw the plaid.

She was wearing a buttoned-up cardigan sweater and one of those pleated kilt-skirts that close with a big safety-pin, and it was the Glenmore all right: not the dress tartan, which is chiefly red, but the hunting, which is light blue and green. Unfortunately, they're doing all kinds of sissy things to the brave old plaids these days—I guess some people feel they're too garish for good modern taste—and these were no longer the honest, bold Highland colors, but the sneaky muted shades so dear to the hearts of the butterfly boys. Still, it was the right pattern and, I was sure, the right girl. At least it was the girl I was looking for. Whether or not she was legally entitled to the name and plaid was another matter.

A musical character in a tailcoat was beating out a Strauss waltz on the piano, using as much body English as if he was battling Tchaikovsky to a draw in Carnegie Hall. The girl was watching and listening, puffing industriously on a cigarette. Her health was her own problem, but I couldn't help thinking that if she had to smoke, she ought to learn to do a better job.

There was some green stuff in a glass on the table. It's been my experience that ladies who go for sweet minty drinks after dinner are apt to be somewhat more objectionable, in a prissy and hypocritical way, than those who slug down a good honest highball, but I won't propose it as an ironclad rule. Nevertheless, my first impression wasn't favorable, and the thought of after-dinner drinks reminded me that I hadn't eaten since noon. Sleep, as opposed to merely employing a bed for its fringe benefits, so to speak, was something that had happened so long ago and far away that I'd forgotten the exact circumstances.

I got rid of a yawn while I could still do it without being rude, and moved forward. The girl looked around and saw me—and knew me, which was interesting. Well, sinister-looking gents six-feet-four aren't too common, and she could have been given a thumbnail sketch at the hotel desk. Or she could have been exposed to a more detailed dossier elsewhere.

"Miss Glenmore?" I said, stopping before her.

The piano player had finished sweeping Strauss under the rug, and was taking a break, so I didn't have to shout. The girl looked at me warily.

"Yes," she said. "Yes, I'm Nancy Glenmore. Are you… are you Mr. Helm?"

"Yes, ma'am," I said, and waited.

She hesitated, and said in a sudden, breathless way, "You'll probably think I'm crazy coming here like this, Mr. Helm—" She stopped.

"So who's prejudiced against insanity?" I said.

It threw her for a moment. Then she licked her lips and said, "Well, I saw a Mr. Walling early this afternoon. I wanted him to do some work for me, but he wouldn't take the job, he just told me a lot of stuff, and then he said he'd already made arrangements to see another member of the family later in the day, and why the devil didn't we all get together? He acted very funny, almost rude, as if… as if he thought I was trying to play some kind of a trick on him, but he did give me your name and London address—" She'd got all this stuff off very fast. Now she seemed to run down abruptly. Her big, greenish eyes watched me for a second or two. Then she went on in the same rapid-fire way: "Well, I just had a wild idea that you might be able to help me. I mean, that we might be able to help each other. You may have something I could use, while I… I may have something you want." Still staring up at me unblinkingly, she added, "To trace the family, I mean."

"Sure," I said. "To trace the family."

There was a little silence. I met her wide-eyed stare with a hard look of my own, and presently her glance dropped, but I didn't really need that token of guilt. Her double-talk spoke for itself. *I may have something you want*, could hardly be anything but a prelude to negotiations for Winnie's release. I felt reassured. Mac had ordered me not to wait too long for contact to be made, not beyond tomorrow noon, but here was my contact already, fiddling nervously with her cigarette and sipping at her crème de menthe frappé. She spoke without looking up.

"It's quite a coincidence, isn't it? I mean, both of us calling on Mr. Walling the same day."

"Yeah," I said. "Coincidence."

"Well… well, it looks as if we're kind of related, Mr. Helm, even if it is a long way back."

I remembered another girl in another country who'd claimed a distant kinship with me once, on another job, and almost got me killed. These ancient family ties, much too remote to bring up any inconvenient questions of incest, can come in very handy for a girl in our line of work—but maybe I was being overly cynical. Maybe she really was Nancy Glenmore, on a sentimental pilgrimage to our ancient Scottish stamping grounds, wearing the tartan as the Crusaders wore the cross. Maybe, but I didn't really believe it.

I said, "That's swell. As a stranger, I'd remain standing politely. As a relative, I'll sit, if you don't mind. I just got in from New York this morning, and it's been a long day."

"Oh, I am sorry!" she said quickly. "Please do sit down."

I sat down. We got the drinks question settled and got a waiter to make it official. I lit another cigarette for her, the first having got itself stubbed out half-smoked, and we sat back and looked at each other with a kind of cautious interest. She was really quite a good-looking girl, in a jumpy and high-strung way. Her face displayed a little too much bone, but it was pretty good bone. Having once used a camera professionally, I couldn't help thinking that she'd photograph well, with her big eyes, strong cheekbones, and clean jawline.

Mentally, however, she was a mess. She had the jitters so badly I wanted to pat her shining dark head in a fatherly—well, cousinly—way and tell her for God's sake to relax.

The waiter put our drinks on the table. When he had gone, I said, "So you talked to Walling? I saw him, too, but he wouldn't help me, either." I kept my voice casual while I slipped her a fast one: "Kind of an antisocial gent, I thought. Kept looking at me through those slaty gray eyes of his like I was a bug on a pin."

She frowned quickly. "That's strange, I had a distinct impression Mr. Walling's eyes were blue."

Well, she'd passed that test. Either she had interviewed the real Walling or she'd been well briefed on his appearance. I shrugged. "The light was behind him. Maybe I made a mistake. Anyway, he wouldn't help me, either. He just referred me to a book in the library."

"I know. *The Scots Peerage*. It seems like a funny way of doing business."

"Uhuh, funny," I said, thinking of a dead man with his finger joints crushed and the back of his head beat in. "So your idea is that we should kind of pool our information?"

"Why, yes," she said, straight-faced. "That is, unless you have some objection."

"Hell, no," I said. "Let's pool. I've got an envelope full of stuff upstairs." I gave her a long, deliberate, appraising look, starting high and ending low. With my eyes on her slim ankles, I said, "Let's go up and look it over." What it probably amounted to, I reflected, was that Basil had had to scramble to find a suitable young lady to play my distant Scottish-American relative—that is, to lead me into the new trap he was undoubtedly preparing for me. He'd had to settle for an amateur, or an inexperienced neophyte. He'd had to brief her and dress her in a couple of hours, and as a result neither the girl nor her getup were quite up to professional standards.

She was nervous and scared, and her clothes were all so new I kept expecting to see an overlooked price tag somewhere. I'd caught sight of the sole of a shoe when she crossed her legs uneasily, and the factory slickness had barely been scratched. She couldn't have more than walked across a couple of sidewalks on it.

"I'll have a bottle and some ice sent up."

I raised my eyes abruptly to her face. She did not meet my glance. She said, "Well, I… I didn't bring my material with me."

I said, "Honey, you brought enough material for me."
She didn't speak, and I said, "Okay, your place then.
Where are you staying?"

"B-Brown's Hotel."

"Sure. Brown's it is. Give me a minute to get my things."

She hesitated uncertainly. I watched her. I'd made
my lewd intentions perfectly clear. If she was just a nice
young lady tourist after all, she'd at least postpone our
genealogical consultation until daylight. More likely
she'd slap my face indignantly and walk out on me.
On the other hand, if she was Basil's emissary, she'd
undoubtedly been told to be as obliging as necessary
to get me where I was wanted. Chastity is not a highly
regarded commodity in our line of business.

After a moment, Nancy Glenmore laughed shakily.
"Well… well, all right, if you're sure…"

"If I'm sure of what?" I demanded.

She drew a long breath. "Never mind. All right. Run
up and get your envelope, Mr. Helm. I'll wait for you in
the lobby."

The doorman had the red Spitfire out front by the time
I got back downstairs. We didn't have far to go, and taking
a taxi would have been easier, but if I was being decoyed
away from Claridge's for a reason, I might be glad to have
my own car handy later. And then again, it might wind
up sitting on the street unattended until the police had it
hauled away, but that was a chance I had to take.

The girl had trouble getting in. You don't walk into a
sports car, you first lower your rump to the seat—they

supply a special grab handle to help you—and then you swing both legs in at once; but she tried to enter left-foot-first and wound up half in and half out, giving us a generous display of nylon before she got herself all tucked inside. She was still rearranging her coat and kilts from the struggle when I got in beside her and sent the little bomb away, making some fine, sharp exhaust noises in the darkening street.

Over the years, Brown's Hotel has been recommended to me by various Englishmen—Les Crowe-Barham for one—as the real place to stay in London. Claridge's, according to these British accommodations experts, is more a museum piece than a hostelry. It had been some time since I'd last visited Brown's, but I found it pretty much unchanged: a slightly less ostentatious establishment than the one we'd just left, with slightly less—but only slightly less—American mink drifting around the lobby like thistledown.

The second-floor room into which we sneaked rather guiltily would have made a good closet for the palatial chambers assigned to Winnie and me at Claridge's. Well, almost. There was still plenty of space for a couple of good-sized beds, a writing table, an overstuffed chair, a couple of straight chairs, a dresser, a wardrobe, and a telephone stand, but if you wanted a morning workout in your room, you'd have to settle for simple setting-up exercises or move some of the furniture out into the hall.

A brand-new suitcase of pale-green molded plastic was open on a stand at the foot of the nearest bed. It had the right amount of stickers and tags on it to have flown, sailed, or swum across the Atlantic. Well, nobody in the business is going to miss out on an obvious detail like that. Elsewhere, closed, stood a smaller bag and a hatboxy sort of case to match, similarly labeled. Some nice new lingerie that did not look as if it had ever been worn showed in the open suitcase. Some nice new bedroom slippers or mules, the sexy kind consisting of a sole and a heel and not much else, stood by the beds.

Since it was getting late, and the Europeans go in for service in a big way, one bed had already been turned back by the maid, ready for occupancy. A long, shiny, pale-green nylon robe and nightgown had been laid out across the foot of it. Seduction-wise, I counted it a point in my hostess' favor. This shortie stuff may be cute, but who wants a woman to look cute in bed? I mean, in the absence of a Lolita syndrome, it's hard to get erotic about a female camouflaged to look like somebody's kid sister. It's practically impossible if she looks like Peter Pan.

Nancy seemed surprised and embarrassed by the intimate atmosphere of her quarters. Anyway, she started forward quickly, as if to smooth out the inviting bed and hang the seductive sleepwear out of sight. Then she caught herself and stopped.

"Just drop your things anywhere," she said.

Her voice was casual, maybe a little too casual, and she'd turned away so I couldn't see her face. Before I could offer to help her, she'd slipped out of her raincoat and hung it in the wardrobe, that massive piece of furniture that is a necessary adjunct to most European hotel rooms, since built-in clothes-hanging space is generally not provided. She turned back to face me. If she'd had any problems with her courage or her conscience, she had solved them very quickly. Her hazel-green eyes were clear and guileless.

"Would you care for a drink, Mr. Helm? I bought one of those customs-free packages they sell on the plane. We could ring for some ice."

I laid my hat, coat, and envelope on one of the straight chairs. "The British drink their whiskey neat, I hear," I said. "Let's not bother the management. If they can do it, I can."

"Well, there's an open bottle of Scotch and a couple of glasses over there on the dresser. Why don't you do the honors while I… while I slip into something more comfortable."

She stumbled a little on the last sentence. I couldn't help glancing at her sharply to see if she was serious. I mean, it's just about the oldest line in the world. Five will get you twenty Eve told Adam to hold that apple just a minute while she slipped into something more comfortable, even though the record shows she didn't have a stitch on at the time. Nancy's face turned pink under my regard. I grinned at her.

"Sure," I said. "I know, your girdle's killing you." I grinned again, wolfishly, and picked up the green nylon stuff on the bed and presented it to her with a bow. "Well, we sure wouldn't want you to suffer a minute longer than necessary, ma'am."

She took the garments, hesitated, and started to turn toward the bathroom; then she swung back abruptly. "Damn you!" she snapped. "You don't have to make fun of a girl just because she hasn't done this corny hotel-room routine quite as often as you have!" She stalked to the wardrobe, disposed of the lingerie, closed the door, and turned again to face me. "All right, Mr. Helm, if that's the way you want it! There's the family Bible and the rest of the papers, right there on the table. You can start researching any time!"

It was kind of like being bitten by a blind, newborn puppy. She'd been all set to go through the usual shabby motions—strong liquor and slinky lingerie and the works—but I'd insulted her by not approaching the situation, and her, with the proper respect. I had made a mistake. I had treated her as an experienced female operative who'd been through the sex bit often enough not to mind having it kidded a little, but she was apparently new enough at the game to take it with deadly seriousness and expect me to do the same.

It made me feel uncomfortable, as if I'd been caught contributing to the delinquency of a minor, but I said harshly, "Cut it out. You know damn well I didn't come up here with Bibles in mind—" I stopped. She did not speak or smile. Her eyes were hostile and unrelenting. I said hastily, "Okay, okay. Don't be mad. Bibles it is."

She hadn't been quite sure I wouldn't get rough, and I saw her face soften with relief as I turned away. I walked over and swung a chair around and sat down at the table with my back to the room. Presently I heard her let her breath out and give a kind of apologetic little laugh as if, since I was going to be nice about it, it wasn't such a grave matter after all. She busied herself at the dresser and came over with two glasses and put one beside me. "There's your drink, Mr. Helm."

"Thanks."

She picked up my manila envelope. "Is this the material you brought? Do you mind if I look?"

"Help yourself."

She took it to the big chair in the corner, and set her drink on the end of the table. I noticed, because it's the sort of thing you make a point of noticing under certain circumstances, that she hadn't tasted it. I picked up my glass, watching her surreptitiously out of the corner of my eye. She was turning on the reading lamp behind her; she showed no reaction whatever. She went on to open the envelope without, apparently, the slightest interest in whether I drank or died of thirst.

Of course, the liquor didn't have to be loaded, this time. She might want to go a little farther toward gaining my confidence—as far as the nearest bed, say—before lowering the boom on me. And even if the drink was drugged, there was nothing for me to do but gulp it down like a good boy and hope I'd wake up in the right place, preferably in Scotland, without too many shackles and bars and bolted doors between me and the girl I was supposed to assist and the man we were supposed to kill.

I told myself to quit stalling, but I couldn't help the

nasty sense of uncertainty you get before you commit yourself irrevocably to a risky course of action. There's always the nagging question: *Have I figured this right?* I couldn't help remembering that Buchanan and several others, who'd probably thought themselves, rightly or wrongly, just as smart as me, had figured wrong. They must have. They were dead. I tried to encourage myself with the thought that each man had lived long enough after being caught to get himself infected with a super-virulent disease, but somehow it didn't make the future look very much brighter.

I nursed the glass in both hands, warming it as if it contained precious old brandy, while I pretended to look over the papers on the table. Then I raised it deliberately to my lips. The girl was examining one of my photostats with absorbed interest. I started to drink. It was the lack of ice, and the stalling I'd done, that saved me. Just as the stuff touched my lips, I caught the faintest hint of a scent rising from the warmed-up liquor that I probably would not have detected if the drink had been cold: a flowery scent that never came from good Scotch, or bad Scotch either.

Incongruously enough, it was the fragrance of violets. It told me what I was dealing with. We'd first encountered this stuff a couple of years before in the possession of a man we'd captured, something nice cooked up by their backroom boys: a colorless, odorless, tasteless liquid completely miscible with water and alcohol. It was volatile enough so that if the medical authorities on the scene didn't take all kinds of precautions and work very fast they wouldn't find much to analyze in the dregs of a drink in an open glass, or the body of a man who had drunk of it. It worked almost instantaneously. They'd called it Petrozin K.

Potentially, it had been a fine weapon for their dirty-works armory, and it had apparently passed all their laboratory tests, but in field use, like so many new products, it had revealed a significant flaw: it wasn't quite stable. Although it had presumably been given all the usual lab-checks for sensitivity to light, temperature, and agitation, when it actually came to be carted around in agents' pockets under normal operating conditions, it started to break down very slightly, and to react with its breakdown products in a peculiar way. It lost none of its potency, but traces of an aromatic contamination were produced—an ester, according to our chemists—that gave it a faint, betraying odor that might, by a romantic individual, be likened to the scent of violets.

Apparently they'd never managed to lick the problem. After six or eight months we started coming up against other unpleasant concoctions and heard no more of Petrozin K. However, an ex-agent of theirs—or a man pretending to be an ex-agent of theirs—who'd fallen into disgrace about that time might still have a little of the older poison in his possession; enough, say, to give to a green-eyed girl to spike a glass, or even a whole bottle, of Scotch.

I managed not to look at Nancy Glenmore, so-called. After all, it wasn't the first time somebody had tried to kill me. It wasn't even the first time somebody had tried to send me to hell by the chemical route. I just hadn't been expecting it tonight. I'd been assuming that, like Buchanan and the others, I was wanted alive, at least temporarily. I guess it wasn't the attempt that shook me so much; it was the fact that, thinking myself clever, I'd almost cooperated in my own murder. Well, the next step was obvious.

I turned slightly away from Nancy and threw my head back as if I were taking a good-sized swallow. I started to set the glass down; then I let it fall with a crash to the floor. I made a thick, strangling noise in my throat, started to rise, and picking a spot uncluttered with broken glass, fell face down on the rug. I thought it was quite a good performance.

There was a brief silence; then I heard a kind of hasty rustling and rattling of papers. That would be my pretty, murderous relative clearing her lap for action.

"Mr. Helm?" she said in a tentative voice, and more sharply: "Mr. Helm!"

I heard her get up and come forward to bend over me. I felt her touch my arm cautiously.

"Mr. Helm. Matthew?" Her voice had turned a bit shrill. "Damn the man, he's passed out! Oh, dear, what do I do now?"

She was obviously playing it safe; maybe she, too, had reason to beware of hidden microphones. She rose again without taking my pulse or testing my eyeball reactions, which was sloppy technique but understandable: she was, as I'd hoped she would, just taking for granted that her lethal stuff had done its work. Now, if I had a bit of luck, she would pick up the phone to report success. Even if she talked in code, it might give me a hint...

I heard a sudden, choked little cry of distress and fear. I opened my eyes. Nancy Glenmore was standing by the table with her own glass, partially empty now, in her hand. She was staring into it with a kind of paralyzed horror. Her mouth was open and she seemed to be trying to breathe, at the same time as she tried to comprehend what was happening to her. Then the glass slipped from her hand and hit the rug and spilled but did not break, and she crumpled to the floor beside it.

When I reached her, she was quite dead.

11

As I crouched by the motionless body, I couldn't help
thinking that it just wasn't my day where women
were concerned. In less than six hours I'd mislaid one
carelessly, roughed one up uselessly—and now I'd lost
one permanently by letting her drink poison right before
my eyes. The fact that my eyes had been closed at the
time didn't really mitigate the error.

Well, with a dead girl before me, that was a hell of
an egocentric way of looking at things. It wasn't Nancy
Glenmore's day, either, and would never be again. She
looked small and broken, lying there, with a wisp of
dark hair trailing across her face and her Glenmore kilts
kind of bunched about her thighs—that damned, muted,
airy-fairy version of the brave old hunting tartan that had
prejudiced me against her from the start. I wondered if I
would have had sense enough to believe her if she'd had
sense enough to dress in the true, old-fashioned plaid.

Because her death made it fairly obvious that her story

had been straight from start to finish. Certainly, if she'd been what I'd thought, an enemy agent who'd lured me here to poison me, she'd have left the liquor strictly alone. There was still a remote possibility that she'd been an enemy agent who'd miscalculated in some way, or who'd been double-crossed, but that was straining pretty hard to account for what she'd done and what had been done to her.

The simplest explanation, and the most likely one, was that she'd been exactly what she'd claimed to be: a tourist kid from the States who'd thought it would be cute to devote her European vacation to family research, in the course of which she'd heard of a distant relative similarly engaged, and had quite naturally looked him up. Probably she'd been feeling adventurous and daring, so far from home, reckless enough to indicate—somewhat nervously and amateurishly, to be sure—that she was available for just about any interesting project, including sexual intercourse, that Cousin Matthew might have in mind.

I'd seen her willing attitude as part of a dark plot because I'd been looking for a dark plot, even hoping for one. But everything that had aroused my suspicion could be explained quite simply as the behavior of an inexperienced young girl, in a travel wardrobe bought new for the great occasion, blowing herself to what she'd hoped would be a giddy, uninhibited, memorable fling abroad, and let the stodgy old morals fall where they might. But she'd come to London at the wrong time, visited the wrong office, offered herself to the wrong man, and now she was dead.

I bent over to sniff at the wet spot on the rug where her drink had spilled, and caught the scent of violets, already fading. I got up and went over to check the bottle on the dresser. Trapped in the corked container, the odor was much stronger. Obviously somebody had slipped in here while she was out and doped her liquor, which brought up the question of why anybody would want her dead.

Well, she'd gone to Wilmot Square. She'd talked to the real, blue-eyed Walling. Almost certainly there was a connection between her death and her visit to this man, who'd subsequently, I remembered, been tortured for information. Apparently he'd told her something or given her something that was a threat to Basil and his cohorts, and after she'd left they'd grabbed him and forced him to reveal what it was.

But on second thought it couldn't very well be anything he'd told her, I reflected. Basil had had that office wired, as indicated by the fact that he'd known enough about Walling's business to impersonate the man very convincingly. Anything Walling had said to Nancy would have been overheard. It had to be something he'd given her, then, something that probably meant nothing to her, but might mean something to me. According to her own statement, she'd announced her intention of getting in touch with me, right there in the office. She'd asked Walling for my London address…

It was as easy as that, showing what a brain can do if you only take the trouble to use it. I found it in her purse: a folded piece of the kind of cheap white paper that comes made up in small pads for scribbling notes on. Judging by its appearance, she'd never even unfolded it. She hadn't needed to refer to it, after all, to remember the name and address Walling had told her.

I opened it up. On it was written: *Matthew Helm, Claridge's*. Below was a hastily scrawled three-word message: *Try Brossach, Sutherland*. I'd found a real clue at last.

I studied it thoughtfully, not to say suspiciously—I don't have a great deal of faith in miracles—and got up and went to the table. The kid had come equipped. In addition to the family information she'd wanted to show me, she'd had maps galore. There were clan maps of Scotland, road maps of Scotland, and even a set of the half-inch-scale contoured Bartholomew maps that require over a dozen sheets to cover the Scottish mainland alone. It made me feel a sense of real loss. I mean, willing young girls aren't too hard to come by, these days, but girls bright enough to know the value of good maps are pretty scarce.

I knew approximately where to look. Sutherland is a county in northwestern Scotland; in fact, it's *the* county in northwestern Scotland. As I studied the map of the right area, somebody knocked on the door. It was a tentative, diplomatic little knock, the kind that might be used by a hotel employee with fresh towels, or by a friend who didn't want to interrupt if anything interesting was going on inside—except that I didn't have any friends in London with the possible exception of Crowe-Barham.

Hastily, I folded the map I'd been looking at and stuck

it into my inside jacket pocket, and a couple of more besides, so as not to indicate too clearly, if I should be searched, the region in which I was interested. The slip of paper I tucked into the top of my sock, which was a little better than putting it into my wallet or wearing it in my hatband, but not much. I'd have preferred to destroy it, but I wasn't quite through examining it yet. The discreet little knock came again. I made sure that all Nancy's belongings were back in her purse, and that the purse was lying on the table in the proper, casual, tossed-aside way. Then I looked grimly at the dead girl on the floor.

Somehow it didn't seem right to drag her into the bathroom or stuff her into the wardrobe. I mean, she was a relative of mine, after all, and she could damn well be allowed what little dignity she'd managed to retain in death. Besides, anybody who was really curious would search the bathroom and wardrobe, anyway. I just pulled out my gun and went to the door, as the knocking came a third time, more sharply and impatiently now.

"Matt," a voice said. "Matthew, darling, let me in."

Even if I hadn't recognized the voice, there was only one woman I knew—in London, anyway—who'd deliberately address me as darling while I was engaged in another woman's room. I sighed, and checked my gun, and put it into my pocket, leaving my hand on it. I opened the door just far enough to let me slip out into the hall.

"Hello, Vadya," I said, pulling the door closed behind me.

She had made a quick recovery since I'd seen her

last. Her hairdo had been reconstructed on a slightly less spectacular scale. Her rumpled suit and damaged blouse had been replaced by a straight black linen dress—well, as straight as her contours allowed—that covered her shoulders but left her arms bare. A diaphanous, multicolored chiffon scarf was strategically arranged to mask the bruises on her neck she hadn't quite been able to cover with makeup. She was wearing the kind of boldly patterned black stockings that were currently making a great fashion hit—I guess every woman has a secret yearning to look like a tart—and high-heeled black pumps.

"It's very thoughtful of you, Vadya," I said. "I certainly appreciate it. But it wasn't really necessary."

She frowned. "What in the world are you talking about, darling?"

"Didn't you come to give me back my coat? I thought you were afraid I might catch cold without it."

"Ah, you are joking me, and your coat is in my room at Claridge's," she said with a laugh. She glanced down at my bulging jacket pocket. "Is that necessary? You should be careful, Matthew, or you will become like those of whom we know, those who cannot even shave without aiming a gun at the man in the mirror and ordering him to stand still."

That took care of the polite preliminaries, and I asked bluntly, "Just what the hell are you doing here, doll?"

"Why, I am following you, of course." Her expression was bland and innocent. "Shall we say that I am protecting my interests? We are working together, are we not? That was agreed. When I see you consulting with another woman, and visiting her room, I am disturbed. That was not agreed."

I said, "Somehow I don't seem to recall all these ironclad agreements."

She smiled. "Perhaps I used the wrong word. Perhaps it was not agreed, merely understood. But we are working together in the matter of McRow, are we not? Despite your lousy behavior of this afternoon, which I magnanimously forgive." She touched her neck lightly, and let her hand fall. "And if there is to be another woman involved, should I not meet her? Who is this girl, Matthew?"

I shrugged. "Just a kid who thinks she's related to me in some way. She asked me up to see her family papers."

Vadya looked at me for a moment, and threw back her head and laughed with real amusement. "You are very entertaining, darling. First it is a wife and then it is a distant cousin. You surely don't expect me to believe—"

It was the reaction I had anticipated. Sometimes the truth can be more useful than a lie. I said, "Hell, believe what you like."

"Matthew, please! I am still not convinced of this marriage and this bride of yours. Don't try to sell me any more of your relations today."

I shrugged. "Okay, so the girl is a desperate Mata Hari type packing a gun in her purse and a knife in her stocking. Have it your way."

"And you will ask me in to meet her?"

I shrugged again. "Sure," I said. "Go on in. Meet her."

I stepped back and opened the door. Vadya rearranged the filmy scarf about her shoulders and walked in. She stopped short. I heard her breath catch. I made a note of the fact that her hand went, not to her purse, but to the top of her dress.

I said, "Be careful. This .38 Special makes an awful mess." I reached back left-handed and closed the door and locked it.

After a moment of silence, Vadya chuckled softly. "We seem to have already played this scene once. Did you kill her, Matthew?"

I said, "Hadn't you better make up your mind? A minute ago you were insisting she was my confederate; now you want to make her my victim. No, I didn't kill her. Did you?" When Vadya didn't answer at once, I said, "Somebody loaded that bottle on the dresser. The kid drank first. That's how I come to be still alive," Well, omitting some details, that was more or less true. I went on, "The poison seems to have been Petrozin K. I believe you're acquainted with the stuff."

"Of course, but it was unsatisfactory. It has not been issued to us for many months."

"You might have had some left in the back of a drawer or the bottom of an old purse."

"Why would I kill her, Matthew?"

I shrugged. "How should I know? But it's kind of a coincidence. I come to London with a wife, and right away the wife disappears, and you're sitting in the lounge downstairs. I meet another girl, never mind who, and immediately she's poisoned, and you're hanging around in the hall outside. And this time there aren't even any extraneous Oriental ladies around to confuse the issue. Could it be that for some reason you want me all to yourself, Vadya? It's a flattering thought. And what did you really come here for, to substitute a harmless bottle for the poisoned one to confuse the police, perhaps?"

Vadya gave the same soft, throaty chuckle. "Your ideas are very ingenious, but look at me, darling. Just look at me. I admit I am a fine womanly figure of a woman in this stupid Dumaire disguise, but surely I am not so well-developed that I can hide a whole fifth of Scotch under my dress. If I came to switch bottles, where is my bottle?" She turned to face me. "And you are being inconsistent, also. If I am getting rid of little girls so I can have you to myself, as you so modestly suggest, would I put poison where you might drink it? I am under orders to work with you, not kill you, Matthew. Until the work is done, you are safe from me."

It wasn't really a watertight argument, but I found myself inclined to believe her, just as a working hypothesis. I guess what I really believed was her involuntary start when she saw the dead girl: she hadn't been expecting that. At least I didn't think she had. I took my hand from my pocket and grinned.

"Okay, Vadya. It was just a notion. I thought I'd better check it out. Well, we'd better get out of here. Just let me pick up my own stuff and wipe off a few fingerprints. No sense making things too easy for the British constabulary—"

I stopped talking and put my finger to my lips. Somebody had been passing in the hall outside. At least I'd thought they were passing, but then the footsteps had stopped. I waved a hand at Vadya. She nodded, reached down to slip off her pumps and, moving very quietly in her stocking feet, on tiptoe, she vanished into the bathroom. I looked around quickly. The dead girl looked convincingly poisoned with her glass beside her. I went over to my own broken glass and arranged myself carefully on the rug, closed my eyes, and started breathing as shallowly as I could.

There was a wait of at least three full minutes, as the person in the hall stood silent, presumably listening. At last I heard the sound of a key being inserted into the lock, and the door opened.

12

It went as smoothly as if we'd rehearsed it for hours. I heard our visitor enter and lock the door again and come forward. I heard him set something on the table. He paused briefly by Nancy's body, and came over to me. I had placed myself so that, because of the table and chair, he had to make his approach from the bathroom side. As he stopped above me, in approximately the right position, I stirred very slightly and let out a feeble moan.

I heard him jump back, startled. There was a quick, predatory movement beyond him, a faint scuffle, a choked-off gasp, and some ugly, muffled, cracking and snapping sounds, followed by a kind of expiring sigh and the sound of a body slumping to the floor.

I heard Vadya's voice: "You can get up now, Matthew."

I rose and brushed myself off. She was calmly putting her pumps back on. The scarf she'd worn about her shoulders now hung from her hand, twisted into a kind of rope. Obviously, it wasn't as fragile as it looked. A man in a dark suit lay face down on the rug between us with a broken neck. He looked very dead. It seemed unnecessarily drastic, but I made no complaint. It wasn't as if the guy had been a particular friend of mine. I did, however, wonder briefly if she'd had some reason for silencing him permanently—or maybe it was just an object lesson to show me that, when it came to garottes, two could play.

I glanced toward the table. A bottle stood there, identical with the one on the dresser except that, presumably, the contents were safe to drink.

I said, "My apologies, ma'am. This character seems to have come to do the switch job I accused you of. Do you know him?"

She rolled him over with her toe, looked at him, and shook her head. "No, do you?"

Her denial sounded convincing, but then, I reminded myself, her denials always did. I regarded our visitor— well, to be accurate, Nancy Glenmore's visitor. He was a big, dark man with a broad, Slavic face. I had seen the face before.

"I won't say I know him," I said, "but I saw him this afternoon. He's the guy who was tailing us in a souped-up Mini when we went for that little spin in Crowe-Barham's Rolls."

Vadya was touching her hair into place. She shook the creases out of her scarf and draped it gracefully about her shoulders again, frowning at the man on the floor. "When you saw him, was he alone?"

"No, but I didn't get a good look at the man with him."

"That means there may still be another nearby. We must watch for him as we leave. But first I think we should take a quick look around."

I made my voice casual: "For what?"

Vadya glanced at me. "Don't be stupid, darling. Maybe this one did come only to switch bottles, but maybe he came to find something, also. He must have had some motive for poisoning the girl, must he not? You search the room and check that purse, there's a good boy. I will search the girl—"

"Leave the kid alone," I said.

There was a brief silence. Vadya straightened up deliberately and swung away from the body on the floor to face me.

"So there was something," she murmured. "And you have it."

"There *was* something," I said. "I have it."

She was a pro. There were a dozen questions she undoubtedly wanted to ask, but she hesitated only a moment. Obviously, I would tell her about it when I damn well felt like it, if I ever did. In the meantime, questioning me would be useless and humiliating. She shrugged.

"In that case," she said, "there is no more for us to do here, is there?"

She walked to the door. I followed her, and let her out. I couldn't help looking back before I joined her in the hall and pulled the door shut behind us. The kid still lay on the floor, in her rumpled, modernized Glenmore kilts.

Beyond her lay the man who was probably most directly responsible for her death. At least his attempted bottle-switch seemed to point toward his being the one who'd planted the poison in the first place. You could call his fate a retribution of sorts, but it didn't really help Nancy Glenmore much.

The slow London twilight was fading when we came outside, having aroused no apparent interest in our progress down the stairs and through the lobby. Nobody followed us away from the hotel. For the moment it wasn't raining, and the streets were drying, but it seemed a little chilly for Vadya in her sleeveless dress. Presumably she was capable of catching cold just like an ordinary woman. My gentlemanly instincts made me turn on the Spitfire's heater for her as we drove away, but I got no thanks for it. She was busy powdering her nose with the aid of the little mirror in her purse.

Presently, she closed the purse with a snap. "There is no sign of the little Austin, but we have a 3.8 Jaguar behind us," she reported. "Three men. Somehow I think it is your British friends. They seem to lean toward honest faces and elaborate transportation."

I had already spotted the black sedan following us. "I'll check with Les," I said. "He did mention having a Jag available, and I want to call him anyway."

"Crowe-Barham?" Her voice held a wary note. "What are you cooking up with him now, darling? Your last cooperative venture wasn't very comfortable for me."

I grinned. "You're a suspicious Communist bitch,"

I said, "and a sadistic one. If you wouldn't go around killing people unnecessarily, I wouldn't have to plead with other people to intercede with the police. Or would you rather have us dodging cops clear to Scotland?"

She glanced at me sharply at this mention of our destination, and was silent. I found a phone and parked beside it. As I closed myself into the booth, I saw that the Jaguar had stopped to wait a block behind us, lights out. I decided they were just a little too conspicuous and obvious to be true. They were being clever. Everybody in London was being clever except me, and it was about time I started.

I managed to figure out the combination of the instrument in front of me—some of those British pay phones have more pushbuttons than an old Chrysler transmission—and I got a secretary on the line, identified myself by name, and asked for Les, as I had done once before that day. This time my request got me a funny little pause, as if I'd said something unexpected. After a bit, a male voice I did not recognize spoke in my ear.

"This is Charles Stark," it said. I remembered being told by Les that a Colonel Stark was his current boss. The voice went on: "We hold these truths to be self-evident, that all men are created equal."

"Yes, sir," I said, making a face at Vadya, who was watching me from the car. Obviously, I'd run into a man who went by the book, silly passwords and all. The Anglo-American identification routine thought up by some brilliant bureaucrat required me to answer the passage from the Declaration of Independence with one from the Magna Carta, and I gave the Colonel a good one: "No taxes, except the customary ones, shall be levied except with the consent of a council of prelates and greater barons."

"Very good, Mr. Helm. Do I understand that you were asking for Crowe-Barham?"

"That's correct, sir." It never hurts to sir them when they have pompous voices and military titles. "Why, is something wrong, sir?"

"We hope not, Mr. Helm," said Colonel Stark heavily. "However, Crowe-Barham did not report in earlier this evening as his schedule required. He has not yet been heard from. When last seen, he was leaving Claridge's in your company and that of a certain lady, if I may misuse the word slightly…"

After I'd finished with the Colonel, I made a quick call to our local relay man, asking him to pass the latest developments on to Washington, along with a couple of questions to which I needed answers. When I got back into the roadster, Vadya was powdering her nose again, keeping an eye on the sedan up the block. She glanced at me rather suspiciously, but asked no questions. That's one thing to be said for dealing with a professional, even one whose motives are undependable and whose politics are deplorable: at least you avoid the yak-yak you'd get from an inquisitive amateur. Vadya started to close the purse as I sent us away.

"Keep it open," I said. "I'm going to try to lose them. Keep me posted."

"Yes, of course." She raised the mirror again. "They just turned on their lights. They are following, about a block behind."

"What did you do with Crowe-Barham?" I asked.

She did not take her eyes from the little mirror. "But really, darling! What dreadful crime have I committed now? Is he missing?"

"Apparently. I was just talking with his boss, a Colonel Stark, who thinks you're no lady."

She laughed. "How ungenerous of the Colonel. But am I then to be held responsible for every person dead and missing in the city of London tonight?… They made that turn. They are still behind us. Two blocks behind now. Drive a little faster. Did Colonel Stark accuse me of having made away with his aristocratic operative?"

"He kind of accused both of us. Anyway, he ordered us to report to his office for questioning, immediately."

She glanced at me. "You do not seem to be rushing in that direction, darling. Not unless they have changed their place of business since I was last informed."

"I take my orders from elsewhere," I said. "I don't suppose you're eager to have a chat with the guy, either."

"Well, not exactly. What makes him think we have harmed poor Sir Leslie?"

"Les is several hours overdue. And he was last seen with us, leaving Claridge's. However, you and I both know he was okay an hour later when he dropped me off. And according to Stark, Les did not take you back to the hotel; at least neither you nor the car were seen there again. And it's not a car anybody's likely to overlook. Rolls-Royces aren't that common, even in London."

Vadya said calmly, "I think you lost them on that turn… Naturally we were not seen to return to Claridge's. Was I to walk in the front door of that so snooty hotel, and through that so snooty lobby, wrapped in a too-big man's coat, with my hair hanging in my eyes and my stockings sagging around my ankles? I had Sir Leslie let me out half a block away, and I slipped into the building by… well, never mind. I may want to use that entrance again some time." She closed her purse. "Yes, they missed us. They just went straight on by the intersection back there. Make a right turn ahead, and then perhaps a left, and I do not think we will see them again. Where would I have got this dress, if I had not been back to my room? Tell Stark to look in 443 and he will find your coat on the bed."

"Sure," I said. "Now break out a map of London, there's one on that shelf under the dash, and tell me how to hit the main highway north."

I heard paper rustle as I drove. Her voice came again: "You said the man we just left dead in that room was following the Rolls-Royce when you saw him earlier. Perhaps this man helped to trap Sir Leslie after I left him."

"Or before you left him," I said.

"What do you mean by that?" she demanded.

I said, "You were in the back seat, and I'd given you back your little gun, remember? Perhaps you held up Les, and turned him over to the driver of the Austin and his unidentified pal, after which your now-dead friend drove you back to the hotel so you could change, while he went on to poison Nancy Glenmore for you. And then you killed him so he couldn't betray you to me."

She laughed easily. "Yes, I am a terrible person, darling. Will you kill me now for my crimes, or will you wait until we reach Scotland? And in the meantime can you tell me the name of this park on our right?... Ah, there is a sign. Now I see where we are. Just keep straight on until you come to a great boulevard, and turn right." She glanced at me. "Well, Matthew? Do I live or die?"

I grinned. "I think that's a very interesting theory I just proposed. I'm quite proud of it. It might even be true. If I find it is, I'll let you know. Meanwhile, just get your hand away from that gun in your brassiere, please, and let me concentrate on my driving."

She laughed again. I felt her relax beside me. After a little, she glanced over her shoulder and said in a different tone, "For a pair of foreigners in a very small car, we certainly made it look easy to lose three local operatives in a fast and powerful automobile, did we not? One might almost think we were supposed to lose them."

"You don't miss anything, do you?" I said. "I think Colonel Stark is being very clever. I don't think he expected us to call him at all; certainly he didn't expect us to turn ourselves in just because we were asked. I think that when Les turned up missing after last being seen with us, Stark had my car located and a beeper planted in it—you know, one of those dinguses that send out a signal to an electronic receiver. Les said his boss was fond of fancy equipment. The Jag was just for show. We were supposed to see it, and lose it, and think ourselves in the clear. Now Stark and his boys can settle down to track us on their radar screens at a safe distance."

"And what do you suggest we do about it?"

"Do?" I said. "Don't be silly. We do nothing. As long as Stark thinks we're leading him in a profitable direction, he'll make sure we have a clear track. We won't have to worry about being picked up by the police, whether for murder or speeding. Sorry we couldn't stop for your things, but I'll buy you a toothbrush in the morning."

Eight hours later we were in Scotland.

13

A driver who knows the country, in a fast, well-broken-in car, can probably make that run in six hours or less, since Britain, like most of Europe, imposes few speed limits on the open road. Missing an occasional turn in the dark, in a brand-new car that had to be babied, it took us a couple of hours longer, and morning twilight was well advanced as we roared through the rolling border country past the neighborhood of Hadrian's old wall, built to keep the savage northern tribes out of peaceful Roman Britain, and entered Scotland at Gretna Green, where people used to go to get married in a hurry, and maybe still do.

Nevertheless, by American standards, it seemed like getting from one country to another in a big hurry. I'd studied maps enough to know, theoretically, that Scotland isn't quite as far from London as Alaska, say, is from New York, but I hadn't quite realized, practically, that you could run clear out of England in a single night's drive. On the other hand, neither had I realized that while it's only about three hundred miles from London to the Scottish border, it's another tough three hundred to the part of the northwestern Highlands in which we were interested.

By the time we reached it, the city of Glasgow was a mess of loused-up, left-handed, early-morning traffic, soaked with rain. Beyond, the country got ruggeder as we proceeded north, the roads got narrower, the weather got wetter, and I got groggier in spite of the fact that I kept Vadya busy pouring me black coffee out of a thermos we'd picked up, along with a bunch of other necessities, like an overnight bag and a few clothes, in a small town where we'd stopped for gas—excuse me, petrol. It's a secret I've managed to keep from Washington so far, but I still occasionally require sleep. I haven't quite managed to kick the habit, although it's not for want of trying.

It didn't help any that pieces had started falling off the car, a characteristic of small British vehicles. They make the most beautifully steering and handling little heaps in the world, but they stick them together with paper clips and old chewing gum. Then they leave a few Rolls-Royces and Rovers standing around, conspicuously to prove that they can put a car together right when they feel like it. By the time we'd fought the daytime tourist traffic up past famed Loch Lomond and Loch Ness, we no longer had windshield washer, temperature gauge, speedometer, or hand brake, and I was starting to wonder when something really essential would let go.

I guess I was paying more attention to these distractions, and to my growing weariness, than to what was going on around me. Anyway, the big Mercedes almost sneaked up on us without my recognizing it as a threat. I mean, we'd established early in the evening that, whatever Colonel Stark and his electronic wizards might be doing—we'd located his beeper, magnetically attached to the gas tank behind the seats, and left it strictly alone—nobody was tailing us in the normal eyeball fashion. We'd discussed the fact that if somebody beat us up from London, or just made a long-distance phone call, we might be picked up when we got into the desolate Highlands where there were only one or two likely roads for the opposition to cover, but the possibility had kind of slipped my mind.

Suddenly there was a big sedan riding our tail and flashing its lights for clearance to pass—in Europe it's taken for granted that some people will drive faster than others, and that the slow drivers will just naturally get out of the way of the fast ones, even if they have to take to the bushes to do it. I glanced at the mirror mechanically, and looked ahead for a suitable spot to let the big car pass on the narrow road. Then I looked more sharply at the mirror.

It was a chauffeur-driven car, with two passengers in the rear. I couldn't tell much about them, back there, except that one was a woman, but under the natty cap that reminded me of our missing friend Crowe-Barham doing his home-James bit, the chauffeur's face had a certain Fu Manchu aspect. And while every Oriental in the United Kingdom might not be trying to kill me, I had a hunch I'd live longer if I acted on the assumption that he was.

I slammed the transmission from fourth into third and

stepped the accelerator to the floor. The roadster jumped ahead with a scream from the gears and a snarl from the exhaust—it was a very sporty-sounding little beast. Beside me, Vadya, aroused by the jolt, sat up sleepily and looked at me. I was glad to see I wasn't the only agent in the world subject to human weakness and weariness.

I said, "You'd better powder your nose quick, honey. You may not get another chance."

The Mercedes, momentarily left behind, was coming up fast. I hurled the Spitfire through a couple of sharp turns without raising my foot—as I say, small British cars may be built fragile, but they do handle well. That gave me a little lead. No ton-and-a-half sedan, no matter how good, is going to take the corners like a sports car half its weight and height. Then the road ran straight for a bit and I had him sniffing at my trunk again, looking big as a charging rhino about to overrun us.

"I think it's Madame Ling in back," Vadya said calmly.

I said, "Hell, every Chinese female is Madame Ling to you. You've got Madame Lings on the brain." I grinned. "You mean the woman actually exists? Congratulations."

"She must have come up from London ahead of us in a big hurry."

I said, "The way I've been nursing this toy along, she could have walked and beat us. Well, I can't hold them off much longer. This damn road isn't crooked enough, and Baby just hasn't got it in the straights, not against a Mercedes. Any guns showing yet?"

"Not yet. But the man in back has shifted over to our

side. He is winding down his window."

I reached down, driving one-handed, and freed my revolver and dropped it into her lap. "Use this. That pipsqueak automatic of yours will hardly shoot through safety glass, and they may have special windows in that fancy limousine. Just one thing, sweetheart."

"Yes?" She had flipped open my gun to check the loads.

"Curb those homicidal impulses," I said. "If you shoot the driver dead, he could yank the wheel the wrong way and come right down on top of us. Just give him a faceful of broken glass to discourage him, huh? You can see blood and brains some other time."

Vadya laughed shortly. "What you really mean is, you do not want that car badly wrecked because your wife may be in it. You think they may have brought her with them from London."

I guess I was really getting pretty tired. The possibility hadn't actually occurred to me, and there wasn't time to consider it now. The road was opening up ahead, and the Mercedes was weaving back and forth behind us, looking for a chance to lunge alongside.

I said, "Okay, I'm opening the gate. Here they come."

Something made a funny slapping sound against the Spitfire's soft top. I heard the simultaneous crack of a gun outside. The bullet came to rest somewhere in the package shelf under the dashboard, right in front of me. That took care of any doubts I might have had about the other party's hostile intentions. I swerved the car violently, to indicate that I was hit or badly scared, leaving the road wide open to our right.

The big sedan shot alongside. Vadya fired twice. Even with the howl of the wind and the roar of the motor, the sawed-off .38 Special made a respectable amount of noise. The side window of the Mercedes went to hell, and a rose of cracks blossomed in the windshield right in front of the driver as the bullets passed diagonally through the forward corner of the car. Momentarily blinded, the chauffeur veered off sharply and hit the bank. In the mirror, I caught a glimpse of the big sedan plowing to a halt, before a curve put it out of sight.

Vadya said, "My hand will never be the same. I think all the bones are broken. What a cannon to carry! Here, I give it back to you... What are you doing?"

I'd swung the roadster onto a dirt track leading off into the gorse or broom or heather, or whatever the local vegetation was called.

"You brought up a certain possibility back there," I said. "I'm going to check it out. Besides, I'd kind of like to know what they intend doing next."

Vadya said, "If you really know the place we want, which you are keeping so secret, why waste time on those people? Better to get there before they reach a telephone and send a warning." Then she glanced at me and laughed. "Ah, you always were sentimental about women, Matthew. Very well, we will go look for your little wife. In the middle of an important case, upon which may depend the fate of the world, we will go hunting for a small, stupid blonde."

I said, "If you never met her, how do you know she's stupid?"

"Any woman who would marry you, darling, cannot be very bright."

Well, I'd left myself open for that. I stopped the Spitfire behind an unidentified Scottish bush and got out stiffly and reloaded my gun while Vadya was climbing out and tying her scarf more firmly over her hair. She'd picked up a boy's black leather jacket and a pair of black sneakers on our small-town shopping spree. They changed her appearance drastically. Although her basic costume remained the same, she no longer looked like a lady of fashion from France, expensively dressed for an evening on the town. She looked more like the kind of black-stockinged beatnik female who'd rush recklessly around the countryside by motorcycle or small sports car.

In the same spirit, I'd got myself a black turtleneck sweater and a sharp-looking cap. A night of hard driving, and some exposure to rain at various stops, had done the rest, giving us both an authentically shabby, wrinkled, tough, and careless look to go with the jazzy, mud-splashed little car.

As we made our way back along the hillside toward a point from which we should be able to get a view of the road and the wrecked Mercedes, I couldn't help feeling that we'd got a long way from London and civilization in relatively few hours. Driving, I hadn't quite realized how wild the country had become, particularly since we'd turned westward off what seemed to be the main tourist trail, shortly after passing through the town of Inverness, at the end of Loch Ness.

With a little sleep under my belt and nothing on my mind I could really have appreciated the scenery around us. Even under the unfavorable circumstances, I managed to notice that it was pretty spectacular. The vegetation was tough and low and windswept, gray-green in color, with few real trees. All around us, steep mountains rose up into the low-hanging clouds. I had to keep reminding myself that we weren't more than a couple of thousand feet above sea level. The place had that high-country feel that you get in the Rockies above ten thousand feet.

We reached our vantage point in time to witness Madame Ling, her associate, and her chauffeur being invited to climb into the cab of a big truck—excuse me, lorry—that had just stopped, or been stopped, at the scene of the accident. The chauffeur held a stained handkerchief to the side of his face; the others seemed unhurt. At the distance, I couldn't make out their features clearly, but I could see that Madame Ling was smaller than I'd expected—I guess I'd visualized a tall, slinky, Oriental menace. Instead I saw a slight little black-haired woman dressed in smart Occidental clothes, including a mink coat that would have bought a lot of oil for the lamps of China. The cab door slammed and the big truck started up and took them away toward the east.

I said, "They'll probably have him drop them off back in Inverness. I don't think it's any use trying to tail them.

They'll be watching for that. How old is Madame Ling?"

Vadya shrugged. "Those smooth-faced yellow bitches have no age, darling. She's over twelve and under eighty. Why, does she attract you?"

"Yeah, like a snake," I said. "I don't like small, subtle women. Big obvious ones are much nicer." Vadya made a face at me, and I grinned and said, "I guess it's safe to go down there now. They aren't likely to double back in that rig. Even if they held a gun on the driver, he couldn't get it turned around on this road."

A bunch of shaggy, black-faced sheep scattered warily as we scrambled down the slope. Reaching the Mercedes, I was surprised at the amount of damage my .38 had done to the window and windshield until I realized that somebody in the Ling party had carefully obliterated all recognizable bulletholes with a rock, to avoid a lot of awkward explanations. On the right side, which had hit the bank, there was a shattered headlight, a bent wheel and front suspension, and some scraped and dented body work. In a way, it was too bad. It was a handsome car.

There was nothing significant inside, just the usual meticulous Mercedes trimmings and upholstery. The keys had been left in the ignition. This caused me a little worry, lest Madame Ling had anticipated our return and set a boobytrap or two, but nothing blew when I took the keys, when I inserted the proper one in the trunk lock, or when I raised the lid. Except for the spare tire and tools, there was nothing in the trunk.

I drew a long breath. I guess I had actually hoped

to find something, or somebody. Well, at least it wasn't totally bad news, like a dead body. I straightened up slowly and looked at Vadya.

"So much for your bright idea," I said. "No blood, no bobby pins, no blonde hairs. Two will get you twenty nobody's been carried anywhere in that trunk, dead or alive."

Vadya moved her shoulders easily under the leather jacket, beaded with fine rain. "It seemed like a logical possibility, darling."

"Uhuh, logical," I said. I took the keys from the trunk and tossed them to her. "Put those back in the ignition, will you, doll?"

As she turned away, I took a small metallic object from my pocket and stuck it onto the metal under the lip of the trunk, before I slammed the lid. Colonel Stark might be a little surprised to find his magnetic beeper attached to the wrong car, but I hoped he'd take the hint, when his homing devices led him here, and check up on the damaged sedan and its owner. With his resources, he'd have a greater possibility of getting something that way than we would, but I wasn't optimistic about his chances. Madame Ling would undoubtedly cover her tracks well.

Still, it left somebody with a clue of sorts to follow, if the two of us should fail. I walked forward and found Vadya leaning far into the car to examine the glove compartment.

"Now, that's a hell of an inviting position for a lady to assume," I said. "Find anything?"

She shook her head, backing out and turning to face me. She looked at me rather sharply, and glanced back towards the closed trunk as if suspecting that she might have missed something, but I saw no reason to tell her what I'd done. Her yearning for international cooperation probably wasn't strong enough to include the British. In fact, I rather doubted it was strong enough to include me, in any permanent way.

That doubt had grown stronger since I'd discovered that the Mercedes trunk had been empty. I mean, it had contained no small blonde girls, living or dead, but it had contained no luggage, either, and none had been transferred to the truck that had taken the Ling party away. And a smart-looking woman like Madame Ling would hardly have visited London without at least one well-filled suitcase.

The implication was that she had not just come up from the south ahead of us as Vadya had been so careful to suggest; instead she'd come driving to intercept us from somewhere right here in Scotland, close enough that she'd seen no need to bring even an overnight bag. Madame Ling might not have been in London, kidnaping people, for months. After all, the only one who positively claimed to have identified her there was Vadya...

14

It was Vadya who suggested that we stop for the night, pointing out that we'd hardly be in shape to cope with any serious problems if we didn't get some rest soon. I didn't believe her reasons, but I didn't argue with her suggestion. The place we picked, although it called itself a hotel, was actually a kind of slant-roofed, two-story mountain lodge, located well off the road in a hollow next to a wide, shallow, rocky, fast-running stream. It seemed to be a dual-purpose hostelry, catering to fishermen in summer and skiers in winter. Several trees grew in the hollow, giving the place a sheltered look by contrast with the bleak surrounding moors and mountains.

There were about a dozen cars in the parking area. Numbers of the black-faced Scottish sheep grazed around the hotel. They were just about the wooliest beasts I'd ever seen, like ambulating haystacks. The nearest ones paused to watch us thoughtfully as we parked and went inside, where a man in tweeds rented us a second-floor room for the night and told us that the bathroom was at the end of the hall, that dinner was already being served, and that we'd get breakfast at seven-thirty in the morning. Here, as elsewhere in Britain, breakfast was included in the price of the room.

I spotted a phone booth at the foot of the stairs and ducked back down to it while Vadya was making use of the facilities down the hall. I had no trouble getting through to our London relay, but when I identified myself in code he gave me the flat wrong-number routine that means get the hell off the line before you can be traced and don't call again.

I hung up and went slowly back upstairs, frowning. In a way it wasn't an unexpected development. Colonel Stark had sounded like just the kind of stuffed shirt who'd lodge a protest through channels against my activities—real and imagined—even while he was having a tracking device planted in my car. I could guess that Mac didn't want to talk with me because, in the name of Anglo-American friendship, he'd been instructed by higher authority to do something he really didn't want to do, namely order me to look up our British compadres hat in hand and offer them my humble services even if it meant letting them have our Dr. McRow for a pet.

It's pretty standard treatment for a tricky official situation. After all, undercover communications are notoriously unreliable, and you can't recall a man you can't reach. I wasn't really surprised at the medicine, it was the way it had been administered that disturbed me.

In my previous message I had asked certain questions. Even if our London man considered his lines unsafe, he could easily have given me a coded hint of where and when I could pick up the information I'd requested. The unqualified cutoff, with no alternative contact suggested, meant that there were no answers available and none expected. I was on my own.

When I re-entered our room, Vadya was standing in front of the dresser working at her hair and making dissatisfied faces at her reflection in the mirror. She glanced at me over her shoulder.

"Where did you go?"

I asked, "Do you want a lie or the truth?"

"Oh, a lie, of course. Lies are always more amusing than the truth. Tell me you went down to lock the car and never even considered using the telephone."

I grinned. She made a final effort toward perfection, grimaced, threw the comb aside, came over to me and put her hands on my shoulders. I was glad to see that she was back in her high-heeled pumps. As far as I'm concerned, women in sneakers can stay on the tennis court where they belong. She looked pretty good for having spent almost twenty-four hours in her clothes. Somehow she'd got most of the travel creases out of the black linen dress, and while the black lace stockings had hit a couple of snags during the day's adventures, the figured stuff apparently didn't run like ordinary nylon, which made it ideal for a lady in our line of work: dark, durable, and sexy-looking. Hose-wise, what undercover woman could ask for more?

With her hands on my shoulders, she looked soulfully into my eyes and said, "I am disappointed in you, darling, I am hurt. Here we are, alone again after two long empty years, but you do not relax for a moment. You plot and plan and sneak off to telephone. Can we not, just for tonight, forget that we are agents and think only of each other and our love?"

I made an admiring sound. "Vadya, you're great. You do that beautifully."

She laughed. "I should. I've had lots of practice. But I'll do it even better after I have had something to eat and drink. Come on, I am absolutely starving."

There's a rumor, started by the French I believe, to the effect that the British can't cook. Being a meat-and-potatoes man from way back, I don't go along with this libel. The liquor laws on the island are incomprehensible, and even when you can legally get a martini it's atrocious, but the food has always seemed more than adequate to my simple taste. I may be slightly prejudiced by the fact that I'm a sucker for the white tablecloths and good service that practically always go with it, even in the remote Scottish Highlands.

Of course, I was being skillfully seduced all through dinner, and that always improves a meal. This was apparently the real reason why Vadya'd had us stop for the night, and she was working at it hard and expertly. She continued to play variations of the basic theme she'd stated up in the room: we were two old pros, doomed by fate to fight on opposite sides, who'd once managed to snatch a moment of rapture nevertheless, and might find another if only we could keep the world and its conspiracies at bay, just for tonight. She was really very good. She almost had me believing that of all the men she'd met in the business, I was the one she always remembered, ever since that night in Tucson.

We practically closed up the dining room, which didn't make it very late, only about nine. There was still pale daylight at the windows when we went up the stairs. As far north as we were, in summer, we could expect only a few hours of real darkness. Back in our room again, I switched on the light, and then went across to pull the heavy curtains at the windows. They seemed to shut out not only the Scottish twilight, but all the world outside.

Vadya was still standing by the door. When I turned back to face her, she made a small adjustment to the fragile-looking scarf she was again wearing about her shoulders—the scarf with which she had killed a man— but she did not move otherwise. I walked across the room and took her in my arms and kissed her. It took a while to do a thorough job. At last she freed herself with a little sigh of satisfaction.

"Ah, that is better," she murmured. "That is much better. I thought you were going to make me do all the work, darling." She looked down, and loosened the scarf, and laid it aside. "Now you can take my dress off. Be careful. It is the only dress I have."

"Sure." I unzipped her and stripped her of one layer of clothing, leaving her clad in a black nylon slip. I performed the operation with great delicacy, as if I were skinning a mink and wanted to be sure to preserve the valuable pelt. I hung the dress carefully in the wardrobe and went back to her. "Yes, ma'am," I said. "One dress removed, intact."

She shook her head. "Matthew, you are being very difficult tonight. Very cynical and difficult. Anyone would think you suspected me of ulterior motives. How do I arouse you to real passion?"

I said, "Keep trying. There's still the slip and stockings. Taking off a woman's stockings—black stockings, yet— ought to affect any normal man the right way. Sit down on the bed and we'll give it a try."

A little anger showed in her eyes. "To hell with you, my friend," she said softly. "I do not think I like you like this."

I said, "And I do not like you like this, doll. Don't be so clever. It's been lots of fun watching you work, but you don't seem to know when to stop. This is your old friend Matt, Vadya. Do you know how long I've been in this business? And still you give me the old please-help-me-off-with-my-dress line, for God's sake, and expect me to go all helpless with desire, or something! Hell, I've pulled dresses off lots better-looking women than you and kept a steady pulse—well, almost steady. Steady enough."

She licked her lips. "What are you trying to say?"

"It's very simple," I said harshly. "I'll be delighted to sleep with you, but don't expect it to get you anything. It's been a long time since an attractive woman got my guard down far enough to profit by it. And she didn't do it by treating me like a gullible boy."

She hesitated. "And… and suppose I did want something from you, how would you suggest I get it?"

I said, "Well, you might try asking."

"Then I am asking."

I reached down and got Walling's note out of my sock and laid it on the table and set an ashtray on top of it to keep it in place.

"There you are. It names a certain place in the county of Sutherland, which starts just above Ullapool, which isn't too far ahead along this road. There are maps in my inside jacket pocket. Number 58 is the one you want. Now can we go to bed and make love like adult people, or do you have some other childish techniques you want to try on me?"

She glanced briefly at the small, folded square of paper under the glass ashtray. Obviously, she was very curious to see what was written on it, almost curious enough to make me wait while she looked, but that would have shown a lack of self-control. The paper was there and would still be there after we'd disposed of the more intimate and urgent business of the evening. She laughed softly and came into my arms.

15

Later, I heard her chuckle to herself, lying beside me in the rather narrow twin bed. I shifted position so I could look at her. There was still a hint of daylight in the room despite the late hour and the heavy curtains. She looked oddly pretty and girlish lying there in the dusk with her hair loose on the pillow.

"What's funny?" I asked.

"You do not act very much like a forlorn bridegroom."

"You bitch," I said fondly. "I should have strangled you while I had the chance. Anyway, I only got married. I didn't join the Boy Scouts."

"Um," she said, unconvinced, but she didn't pursue the matter further. I heard her sigh. "It is really too bad."

"What is?"

"You know I have orders to kill you."

This was supposed to startle hell out of me. I grinned and said, "By this method? I can't think of a pleasanter way to go."

She laughed. "Oh, you are not to die until you have served us well, of course. And not at all if it interferes with more important business. But you have annoyed some of our higher people for a long time, and they would like me to dispose of you when this job is finished, if it is not too much trouble."

"And in the meantime you're telling me all about it?"

"Of course. You are not a fool; you have already considered the possibility, I am sure. So now I tell you about it with great frankness, and that makes you think I do not really mean it very much; that I am only talking to shock you. It is very good technique."

I said, "In that case, I'd better tell you that my boss has kind of hinted that it would be nice if I got rid of you, too, if it's not too inconvenient."

She smiled, and stopped smiling. She murmured, "And the terrible thing is that we will do it, will we not? No matter what has happened between us, in the end we will both try to carry out our instructions."

"That's right," I said. "What happens in bed means nothing anywhere else. It's something the suckers never remember, and people like us never forget."

"Of course." She hesitated. "Matthew—"

"Yes?"

She drew a long breath. "Never mind. Turn on the light, please. I am going to look at your piece of paper."

"Don't bother," I said. "I can tell you what it says. It's a note from a gent named Walling, to me. It says, *Try Brossach, Sutherland.*"

"Brossach?"

"That's what it says."

"And why would this… this Walling send a note to you?"

"I never talked to him alive, except on the phone, so I can only guess. But I figure he'd spotted my predecessor, a guy going by the name of Buchanan, as an American agent. At least Walling had spotted Buchanan as a fake, and later read that he'd died mysteriously. Walling made a couple of shrewd guesses. When I called up with practically the same line, Walling jumped to the conclusion that I'd been sent to follow up the case. Just like your people figured when they saw me in London."

"And had you been sent to follow up the case?"

I grinned at her. "I told you. I just came over here on my honeymoon, nothing else. I'm strictly an innocent bystander, dragged into this mess against my will, but I can't seem to make anybody believe it." I shrugged. "Anyway, Walling was looking for help. He was scared. His partner had been run over by a truck, and his secretary had come down sick, and he had a hunch he was next, as he was. But he got the word out by Nancy Glenmore before he died." I glanced at Vadya. "And don't give me that know-nothing routine. You've been told all about Walling. And a lot about Buchanan, probably."

"Yes, that is your man who was found right up here near Ullapool."

"Correct. There's something funny about that. If they really have their headquarters in this vicinity, you wouldn't think they'd call attention to it by leaving dead bodies lying around."

"They have left other dead bodies around. With warning signs on their bodies. Not to mention people who have disappeared and never been found. There have been quite a number of those."

"But there wasn't any warning sign on Buchanan's body," I said. "That's my point. If he hadn't been found by a tweedy doctor type on vacation, who didn't like the medical aspects of what he saw, McRow's super-plague might already be loose in the land. And those other cases all happened back while McRow and his patrons were still showing us what they could do, and while their operation was small and handy enough that it could easily be moved whenever anybody got close. But I have a feeling this Scottish station is the last stop on the line. I think they're now set up for production rather than research, and they want to defend their privacy at any cost until they've stockpiled all the stuff they need to force the world to pay up, if that's really what they're after."

Vadya glanced at me sharply. "You do not think that is what they are after, Matthew?"

"Well, it's a hell of a big deal for just a spot of blackmail," I said. "They could just be spreading that notion around to keep us and McRow quiet, thinking that we know what's coming, and that we'll have plenty of time to answer their demands when they're made." I shrugged. "I don't know. In any case, if this is the critical stage of their operation, they wouldn't have let Buchanan be found anywhere close if they could have helped it. I think he just got away from them, which is encouraging. If one man can get in and out of the joint, another can. Maybe even without contracting a fatal disease." I hesitated. "There's one thing that bothers me, though. If this is Madame Ling's baby, why didn't she just haul McRow back to the land of the dragon for the final step. They'd all have been safe there."

"Safe?" Vadya laughed shortly. "That is not our information. We are told that your crazy scientist's process is not really safe anywhere. And if something should go wrong with a thing like this, Madame Ling's superiors would undoubtedly rather have it go wrong half a world away from their own sacred personages."

"Well, that makes sense," I said. There was something familiar about the scene. I seemed to be forever holding serious war councils in bed, with women I'd just made love to. Well, I couldn't think of pleasanter circumstances. I went on: "But it must be pretty tricky if they don't even want it brewing in Outer Mongolia."

Vadya said, "They are probably very much aware that they are really the last people in the world who should be meddling with biological weapons. After all, the best targets for disease in the modern world are the crowded and underprivileged populations of Asia." She frowned at the ceiling. "Brossach? It is a strange name. Where is it, darling?"

I grinned at her. "Hell, if I knew that, sweetheart, I wouldn't be confiding in you."

Her eyes narrowed quickly, and she turned her head to look at me. She started to speak, changed her mind, threw back the covers, got out of bed, and switched on the light. I watched her walk over to my coat, hanging on a straight chair. She took the maps from the inside pocket and, as an afterthought, threw the coat over her shoulders since the room was cold and she had nothing on. The effect was quite intriguing, but she made no attempt to capitalize on it. She just got the slip of paper and glanced at it to make sure I had quoted Walling's message correctly; then she spread the right map on the unused bed and started scanning it carefully.

I said, "You're wasting your time. It isn't there. I've looked. Furthermore, our research people can't seem to find it. I called them from London the other evening when I talked with Stark—you remember—and I checked with them again tonight, but they had nothing for me." That was true enough, even though it implied better communications than I'd actually been able to establish. I went on, "If they haven't been able to find it in twenty-four hours, God only knows how long it will take them. I'm guessing it's a specialized local reference of some kind, too ancient or insignificant to appear in the usual atlases or histories."

"Walling knew it," she said without looking up from her examination of the Bartholomew map.

"Walling was a trained and experienced genealogist. It's possible that if we went through his library carefully, we'd find it mentioned in some beat-up old edition of some obscure and privately printed little genealogical monograph that Washington never heard of—" I stopped. Vadya had turned away to the overnight case we'd bought. She was pulling out a pair of new black pants and a new black jersey. "Where are you going?" I asked.

"To the telephone. I will get our people on it."

I said, "To hell with that. That's just more time wasted."

"What do you mean?"

I said, "Give us a little credit, Vadya. If an American research unit can't track down an old Scottish name, what makes you think a bunch of your Russian experts can?"

"We have a very good organization," she said stiffly.

"Sure. So do we. So do the British. And if we're going to go the research route, our best bet is to get Colonel Stark on it. After all, it's in his back yard, he's undoubtedly got people who know Scotland intimately, and furthermore he's got access to Walling's place. Since the murder, there's probably a cop at the door, so none of our people—yours or mine—can get in without shooting their way in, which won't give them time for much library work afterward, before more cops arrive."

She hesitated. "I am not authorized to cooperate with the British."

"I didn't think you were. And I'll admit we don't quite see eye to eye with them, either." I grimaced. "If you're going to put those clothes on, for God's sake put them on. The suspense is killing me."

She laughed in a preoccupied way, and climbed into the trousers, squirmed into the jersey, and came over to me pulling it down about her hips. Without Madame Dumaire's artistically padded foundation garment, now part of a careless heap of clothes on the other bed, her figure was considerably less voluptuous than it had been, but she still wasn't really constructed to be at her best in pants. But then, no woman is.

"Turn around," I said, and I picked a price tag off her rear. "Fifteen shillings, sixpence? For a strong healthy girl with good teeth, it's a bargain."

She didn't smile. "I am getting the impression you brought me along for a purpose, Matthew. What is it?"

"What a silly question," I said.

"Stop it. Our love is a beautiful thing, no doubt, but it could have been consummated just as readily in London. Be serious, darling."

"Sure," I said. "Sex apart, I did kind of figure I might have some use for you up here. I hoped our research people could get me the necessary information. That would have been the easy way. Now we've got to do it the hard way."

"Tell me."

"Well, it occurred to me that you're a lousy Red Communist agent, Vadya. And Madame Ling is a lousy Red Communist agent. And that gives you two lovely ladies something in common. I would say the differences between you aren't insurmountable. Are you following me?"

She was silent for several seconds. Then she said, "Yes, I think so. Go on."

"Madame Ling," I said, "is probably sitting in Inverness right now, acting like a rich foreign tourist waiting for her car to be fixed. After being caught off base, so to speak, she won't dare rush back to HQ, wherever it is—call it Brossach—without first making foolproof arrangements to make sure she won't be followed. Well, there can't be too many hotels in a little town like Inverness good enough for Madame Ling; she looked like a fastidious sort of person. You shouldn't have a great deal of trouble reaching her by phone."

Vadya said carefully, "I killed one of her men in London. At least I suppose he was one of hers, although he wasn't Chinese."

"I never heard of Peking getting particularly upset over the loss of a little low-class manpower. You did it to protect yourself, and to gain my confidence, of course."

"I helped put her car in the ditch."

"But you didn't shoot to kill. Not when you saw who was in the car. It was unfortunate, but you're not obliged to let yourself be wrecked, even by a fellow-believer in the doctrines of the great god Marx."

She said quietly, "You are not being very polite, darling. I do not sneer at George Washington in your presence."

It was no time to laugh, and maybe old George was as good a patron saint as any. I could certainly use all the help I could get, and he'd been a pretty competent guy in his time.

"My apologies," I said. "Strike it off the record."'

"What do you want me to tell Madame Ling?"

"Tell her?" I said. "Hell, that you're ready to sell me out, what else?"

There was a little silence. Then she said, "Go on."

"Why else would you have gone to the trouble of gaining the confidence of, and pretending to cooperate with, a nasty bourgeois type like me? You've been keeping an eye on me to make sure I did no harm to the great common cause—also, admittedly, you've been trying to find out for your superiors in Moscow just what their good friends to the east are up to. But now you figure it's time for all good proletarians to join forces and, as a first step, to wrap me up and put me in the deep freeze before I have a chance to get really troublesome. Of course, you expect a little information in return for your help, maybe even a guided tour, so you can make your report to the home office look good."

She hesitated and said dubiously, "Matthew, I—"

I said, "It's a cinch. You get the drop on me convincingly, and turn me over to them. If you work it right, they'll take us both inside, me as a prisoner, you as a trusted—well, more or less—ally. When the time comes, you help me get free and we go after McRow together, just the way we worked it in Mexico. Remember?"

"Yes," she said. "Yes, I remember." She picked up the map and started to fold it thoughtfully; then she looked back at me, having made up her mind. "You will have to trust me, darling," she said.

It was as good a tipoff as a flashing red light and a warning rocket. Whenever they start talking about trust, they're going to double-cross you. Well, I'd thought she'd see the possibilities, all of them.

16

In the morning, when we came outside for breakfast, the sun was shining. A few spectacular white clouds still hung over the mountains that edged the high valley or bowl in which the hotel was located, but elsewhere the sky was as blue as you could wish.

The sunshine turned the treeless moorland scenery from bleak to beautiful. It was really a hell of a fine, wild-looking country, and I wished I could go hunting in it, or even fishing, although I haven't got quite enough sadism in me to really enjoy fishing. I can rationalize killing a living creature quickly, with one well-placed shot—after all, we connive at death every time we order steak—but letting it fight its heart out against a nylon leader, and then boasting about its game, despairing struggles over a beer afterwards, is a little too specialized a form of amusement for my simple soul.

Vadya said, "Someone has been in the car, Matthew."

We had, of course, arranged the usual system of

telltales to let us know if our transportation had been tampered with. I stopped admiring the view and checked the trunk and hood. Neither had been opened. The wheels had not been moved or lifted. Since it was a very low-slung little car, this made it reasonably safe to assume that nothing fancy had been hung on us underneath. But the left-hand door had definitely been opened.

I said, "Maybe Stark's boys came to get their beeper." That would explain its disappearance, if Vadya should notice.

She frowned. "Or maybe somebody has arranged to blow us up as we get in. After my phone call last night, Madame Ling knows where we are, and I don't have a great deal of faith in that little yellow slut."

"What a way to refer to a fellow-believer!" I said. "And I thought you people were always reproaching us for our racial prejudices… Well, it's easy enough to check, in a roadster."

I unsnapped and unhooked various fastenings and managed to work the cloth top free without disturbing either door. Sports car tops do not come down hydraulically at the touch of a button. They have to be dismantled piece by piece, folded, and put away by hand. At least this is true of the tops of inexpensive British sports cars. Having uncovered the cockpit, I examined the interior, and found nothing. I grasped the handle bravely and pulled open the suspect door. No explosion resulted.

I grinned at Vadya, who'd instinctively stepped back. "Well, now we've got it off, on this lovely morning, we might as well leave it off," I said, and I stowed the framework in the trunk and folded the top carefully so as not to further damage the plastic rear window, which already displayed a bullethole as a reminder of yesterday's adventures. "What are you doing?" I asked.

Vadya was kneeling on the seat. There was a narrow luggage space behind. At the back of this was a removable panel leading to the gas tank compartment, which also served to hold the folded tonneau cover, and any other small items you cared to tuck out of sight. She had the compartment open before I could distract her.

"Just checking," she said. "No, they didn't get it."

"Who didn't get what?"

"Stark's boys didn't get their beeper. It's still here."

She picked it off the metal to which it clung magnetically, and showed it to me on her palm. It was the tiny British homing device, all right, identical with the one I'd sneaked out of there yesterday and left in the trunk of Madame Ling's wrecked Mercedes.

I managed to conceal my surprise. For a moment I wondered if Vadya, or Madame Ling, was being very tricky; then I realized that I had simply underestimated Colonel Stark. The man had brains after all, and even a sense of humor. He'd found the beeper in the Mercedes, and then he'd had it—or another just like it—put back in my car in exactly the same place as before. This got me off the hook if Vadya should investigate, as she'd just done; it also told me that my message had been received and appropriate action was being taken.

Vadya said, "I think it's time we got rid of this, don't you? We don't want interference by the British."

Before I could give her an argument—I couldn't think of a plausible one—she'd thrown the little transmitter into the nearby stream. Well, I wasn't too eager to have Stark right on our tail myself, but I found myself feeling a little more hopeful about the guy. He might turn out to be of some use eventually.

I closed up the compartment, and set the overnight case behind the seats, along with a picnic lunch supplied by the hotel, and our thermos bottle, refilled. If everything went according to plan, I wouldn't be at liberty long enough to do much eating or drinking, but I couldn't let it look as if I were anticipating captivity. The sandwiches and coffee indicated, I hoped, that I was innocently looking forward to a full, energetic, outdoors day spent searching for a place called Brossach.

"Give me course and speed," I said as we drove away, "and estimated time to target."

"Turn right when you reach the highway," she said. "Go on through the town of Ullapool and several miles further—she didn't give me the exact mileage—and turn left toward the coast on a little one-track road. The sign is supposed to say Kinnochrue. They'll be lying in wait for us somewhere on that road."

"Sure," I said. "Well, let's hope they make it good. I have a reputation of sorts to maintain; I can't just fall into their arms or they'll know it's a plant." I paused to give the right of way to a couple of shaggy sheep, and swung the Spitfire onto the main road. Presently I glanced at the mirror and said, "Well, there's one of them already.

Our little tan Austin-Cooper from London, with only one man aboard. He must have had a long, sad, lonely ride up here, grieving for his lost friend, the guy you finished off in Nancy Glenmore's room. I guess he's supposed to shepherd us into the trap."

Vadya had her purse open and was studying the mirror inside. She said, "I don't recognize him. He is too far away."

I said, "Quit your kidding, doll."

She laughed softly. "Very well. I do recognize Basil, although I never did know him well. I guess I was just... well, ashamed to admit that we have people like that, self-seeking, ambitious, and cowardly."

"I never heard that Basil was yellow."

"He did not have the courage to keep faith with the Party!"

"Oh, that," I said.

"Furthermore, he did not have the courage to die in a situation that required his death. The details do not matter—it was hushed up, of course—but that is why he became a traitor. He knew that his career with us was finished so he switched his allegiance elsewhere; now, finally, to the Chinese. A cheap, dirty little turncoat, but well trained and quite clever. Do not underestimate him."

"I'm not likely to," I said. "He made a sucker of me in London. Almost a dead sucker, or a kidnaped one." I glanced at her, and said, "Talking about kidnappings."

"Yes?" Her voice was cautious.

"You have Winnie, don't you?"

After a moment, she glanced at me. "Yes. I have her."

"Aren't you ashamed of yourself? Framing poor Madame Ling like that? Where'd you get the woman to impersonate her?"

"As you said yourself, an Oriental stooge is no harder to find than an Occidental one, in a cosmopolitan city like London. As you also said, I wanted you to myself, but of course you could not be permitted to know I had arranged it, so I threw the blame on Madame Ling." Vadya laughed. "I did not think I could get as much… cooperation from you, if you had a wife along."

"And the kid, Nancy Glenmore? Did you have her disposed of, too. For the same reason?"

Vadya was not offended by the question. She merely shook her head. "No. Basil must have ordered that. I might very well have done it, but I did not. And your little blonde playmate is quite unharmed and will be released as soon as I can get word to the people who hold her. Are you angry?"

"Sure," I said. "I'm mad as hell I let you out-bluff me when I had that strap around your neck."

She laughed. "You are a sentimentalist, my dear. I knew you would not kill me, or even hurt me badly, no matter how threateningly you talked."

I grinned. "Crowe-Barham wouldn't agree with your opinion of me. He thinks I'm an uncouth Yankee brute. If he's still alive, poor guy. You didn't happen to get any word on him from Madame Ling?"

We hadn't discussed the details of her telephone conversation the night before. Sleep had seemed more important, once she'd let me know that contact had been established and satisfactory arrangements made.

Vadya said, "No, even if I'd thought of it, how could I have asked? What interest could I have in your friend? I merely made my offer, we haggled a little over terms, and she consulted her associates and came back to the telephone to let me know what I was expected to do. When we stop, of course, I will point my gun at you."

I said, "Sure. But be damn certain you don't do it before we stop, or I'll have to go through the motions of piling up the car, or doing something equally desperate and messy."

What I meant was that it's only on TV that a guy in a fast-moving vehicle, with a steering wheel in his hands and a hot engine under his foot, lets himself be held up by a character with a mere pistol, who obviously can't shoot since if he does his victim will be sure to wreck the heap and take him to hell for company.

"I will wait," she said. "Then I will get your revolver. Then they will come up and take you prisoner."

I asked, "Did the Ling make any provision for communicating with you again if something went wrong?"

"Nothing is supposed to go wrong. But she gave me an emergency number to call, yes."

"And just how are you supposed to be selling this lonely coastal detour to me?"

"Why, I called our people in London, did I not? And they were very efficient—much more than yours— and discovered that the Kinnochrue road goes on past Brossach, which is a very old castle, crumbling into the sea, only a few stones left on the edge of the cliff. It was the ancient home of the clan McRue, destroyed in one of those bloody Highland feuds you read about. Since this obscure clan died out long ago, and since there is not enough of the castle left to attract tourists, and since it is a long way from the road and the cliffs are not safe, hardly anybody knows about it. So said Madame Ling, pretending to trust me with important information. I am fairly certain that Brossach is not on that particular road, and it may not even be an old castle on a cliff, but that is what I was told to tell you."

I said, "Well, with luck they'll take us there, wherever it is. I'm glad we came across the Ling when we did. Or she came across us."

"What would you have done if she hadn't?"

I shrugged. "They knew I'd got information from Walling, and they didn't know I didn't know what it meant. As long as I headed in the right direction and looked as if I knew where I was going, they were bound to try to stop me. We couldn't help but run into somebody you could make your treacherous offer to, somewhere along the line."

She laughed and patted my arm. "Darling, you are an ingenious man and a good poker player, even if you are sentimental about women."

I opened my mouth to warn her not to count too much on my famous sentimentality; then I closed it again. If she wanted to keep thinking I was a soft-hearted slob, that was her privilege.

17

I had been warned about the one-lane roads of the real Scottish hinterland, and the courtesies and conventions governing their use. They are, for the most part, smoothly paved and well maintained, but they are barely wide enough for a single car—just narrow little tracks of black asphalt winding through the rocks and heather.

At intervals, there are passing places marked by white, diamond-shaped signs set high on tall posts for better visibility. If a car comes up behind, you are supposed to pause at the next passing place and let it pull around you. If one approaches from ahead, you are expected to wait at the next passing place for it to go by, unless it reaches a diamond first and waits for you.

We'd come through Ullapool, a picturesque but tourist-infested fishing village on an inlet called Loch Broom, where we'd had our first glimpse of salt water on this rugged western shore of Scotland. Beyond, the main road had swung inland again, and presently we'd seen the sign pointing to Kinnochrue and made our left turn, followed faithfully by the squatty tan Austin-Cooper.

Now I was ramming the Spitfire hard along the twisting black track through the coastal hills. I was kind of testing the skill of the guy behind and the capabilities of his chunky little sedan. I had to admit that while my streamlined red roadster looked a lot faster, I didn't really have much if any edge, mechanically speaking, and Basil seemed to be a pretty good driver. Well, they're all pretty good until the chips are down; then some get suddenly better and a few get suddenly worse.

I put my foot down harder. The exhaust began to sound raucous and impatient, the wind started buffeting us in the open cockpit, and the tires whimpered in the curves. Basil began to fall back. Of course, there was no real need for him to take chances. He couldn't lose us on that road; there was no place for us to go. Still, it looked as if he just didn't have the urge. I could see why he'd had another man to handle the car in London. He could drive, but he wasn't a *driver*, if you know what I mean. His machinery could catch me, but he never would.

Vadya said tartly, "I hope you are enjoying yourself, darling." She had to speak loudly to make herself heard over the noise.

I glanced at her and grinned. "What's the matter, are you scared?"

"Of course I am scared," she shouted. "You are driving like a fool, and I have no particular desire to die."

"Neither does he," I said, jerking my head backwards.

"Which is what I wanted to find out... Ooops!"

I hit the brakes and swerved into a providential passing place barely in time to miss a big Morris sedan that had appeared out of nowhere—at least it looked big on that skinny little road. Then we were off again, while Basil had to wait at a passing place up the line for the larger car to go by. That gave us an additional lead as we charged the next rise hard enough to feel the car kind of lift as the road dropped away beyond the crest—and there they were.

They must have had somebody on a height to give the signal we were coming; they were already busy setting a Volkswagen Microbus crosswise down there. It was plenty big enough to block the road completely. On either side, the shoulders dropped off into rank, soggy-looking grass and brush studded with occasional nice big boulders.

In a jeep, or maybe even a rugged American pickup truck with plenty of clearance and low-gear pulling power, I might have considered an end run nevertheless. In a fragile, low-slung sports job with high-speed gearing, it was out of the question. Even if I got it down from the road intact and right side up, I'd never get it back to the pavement again beyond the roadblock. It would either sink belly-deep in the peat bog or disembowel itself on a rock.

They'd seen us now. The driver of the bus had set his brake and was running for cover, and there were a couple of men on either side of the road, waiting to close in on us when we came to a halt. But between them and us was a white diamond on a post, marking a rather skimpy passing place.

I said, "Hang on, doll. This may work. If it doesn't, it will still look as if I'd given it the old college try."

She said something that I didn't catch. We were really flying down the narrow strip of pavement now. All you could hear was the scream of the exhaust and the howl of the wind. The passing place was coming up fast. At the last moment I stood on the brake and rammed the gearshift lever into low. As we came sliding up to the wide spot, while we still had momentum, I got off the brake, cranked the wheel all the way over, and hit the accelerator hard.

It's a trick we used to play long ago, in our folks' flivvers, on snowy roads back home. If you swung the heap hard and really goosed it, you could skid it around in its own length. If you chickened out, you wouldn't spin far enough, and you'd jump a curb or clobber a couple of parked vehicles. If you hit it too hard, you'd do a complete three-sixty, and go sliding on down the street, spinning end for end. But if you did it just right, you'd have made a neat U-turn using hardly any street at all.

This wasn't snow, of course, but I saw a little gravel in the turnout that might help, and the Spitfire had a much smaller turning circle, and a much faster steering ratio, than the cars I used to play with. After all, I'd picked it for its spectacular maneuverability; now was the time for it to show its stuff.

For a moment, however, it seemed as if we'd go flying off the bank and out into the rocky field: I couldn't break the rear wheels loose. The car simply tracked around tightly, shuddering and protesting, in a circle that, small as it was, was several feet too wide for the space we had. Then the straining rear tires hit the gravel and went sideways with a jerk and we were spinning nicely. The tail of the car whipped completely around. I caught it at a hundred and eighty, overcorrected and almost lost it, and fishtailed wildly before getting it back under control. Then we were heading back up the slope.

Basil was not yet in sight. We came over the crest again, turning about five thousand in third gear—about fifty m.p.h.—and saw him just approaching the passing place that we'd used to avoid the Morris. I suppose I should have let him reach it, but I remembered a girl who'd died of poison, probably at his orders, and I saw no good reason to be nice to Mr. Basil. Besides, sitting in an open car, a perfect target, I had to keep him too busy to use a gun until we were out of range. He might shoot better than he drove.

I raced him for the white diamond, therefore, taking the revs clear up to six thousand before I grabbed high gear. He wasn't a real driver, as I've said. He couldn't see that if he slowed down, he was lost. He *had* to reach the wide place first, if he wanted to avoid a real sudden-death showdown, but still he tried to hedge his bets and make the crash a little less terrifying if it should come.

"Chicken!" I heard myself shout like a crazy kid. "Get off my road, chicken!"

I was aware of Vadya glancing at me, presumably contemptuous of this childishness. Basil couldn't hear me, of course, but he eased off irresolutely nevertheless;

and the passing place flashed by us. He'd lost the race, and now the red Spitfire was hurtling at him downhill at seventy-five, crowding eighty, wide open, and there was no room for him to dodge on that one-track road, and nothing left for him to do but ditch or die. He ditched.

I had a glimpse of the Austin going over the edge as we roared past. I drew a long breath and carefully let the roadster slow down, and I looked at the steering wheel to see if I'd actually squeezed fingermarks in the hard plastic. I hadn't.

I said, "Some bottle, with a coward for a cork. Did he crack up hard, I hope?"

Vadya said calmly, "Unfortunately, not too hard. He was not going very fast. The car bounced a couple of times and hit a big stone and fell over on its side. I think it is seriously damaged. But he was getting out when we turned the corner." She glanced at me. "What would you have done if he had not got out of our way, Matthew?"

"Hit him head on," I said, "and he knew it."

We drove in silence for a little, and then she said softly, "You are a surprising man in many ways, darling. Or are you just a reckless boy? And do you not care at all whether you live or die?"

I said, "Hell, everything indicated that he'd weaken if I came at him hard enough. Look at his record. The only real risk was that he might panic completely and freeze at the controls. I wouldn't have tried it on you. You're too stubborn. You'd have hung on and got us all killed, out of pure meanness."

She laughed, and pulled her scarf off her hair, and used it to pat her forehead. "I do not know, darling. I am not so sure. You were bluffing in London, but you were not bluffing here." She sighed. "Well, what do we do now?"

I shook my head ruefully. "That wasn't much of a trap. I couldn't let them get away with it. Madame Ling either has a very low opinion of me, or she was testing me to see if, perhaps, I really wanted to get caught. It looks as if you're going to have to call that emergency number. Bawl her out. Tell her I don't really suspect anything yet, but she'd better make her next setup good." I looked around, seeing no landmarks, nothing but rocky hills, and a few sheep. The sheep over here had white faces, I noticed. They didn't have the sturdy, independent, go-to-hell look of the black-faced ones. I said, "Well, we'd better hunt up a phone. I don't see any booths around here."

Vadya had the map out. "Kinnochrue should be the closest place from which to call. There's another road we can use. Turn left up ahead."

I followed her directions mechanically. I was feeling a little drained, I guess, as the adrenalin wore off; you get yourself all keyed up to put your life on the line and there's bound to be a reaction afterwards. Presently I found myself negotiating a small dirt road on which the Spitfire scraped bottom no matter how hard I tried to maneuver around the high spots. It got progressively worse. At last I pulled off to the side and turned off the engine.

"As a navigator," I said, "you make a swell secret

agent. Let me see that map. Where the hell are we? I mean, where the hell do you think we are?"

She put her finger on the map. "I think we are here, darling."

"Nuts," I said. "We haven't crossed the main highway, have we? I'd have noticed that."

I got out to stretch and spread the map on the hood of the car—the bonnet, in the local parlance. There was a rustling of waxed paper in the car; I looked up to see Vadya munching a sandwich.

"Want one?" she asked.

"No, but I could use a cup of coffee."

She brought it to me, and reached up to pat my cheek lightly. "You're a funny man, Matthew. *Chicken*, you shouted, *get out of my road, chicken*. Your road! What arrogance!"

I said, rather abashed, "I got a little carried away, I guess. I—" I looked beyond her. "My God, what's that?"

She whirled, putting her hand to her bosom where her little gun, apparently, still reposed. Then she let her hand fall, and we stood looking at the fantastic creature that had appeared on the ridge to the west of the road. It was big as an ox—in fact it was an ox, but like no ox you ever saw. It had long, shaggy, ragged, yellow-orange hair, and great, spreading horns like an old-time trail steer. It looked at us calmly for several seconds before it turned and moved deliberately out of sight.

I glanced at Vadya, and we scrambled up there like two kids at a zoo, rather than two ruthless secret operatives on a mission upon which might depend the fate of the Western world. We stood watching the great beast walk slowly away from us, hairy and prehistoric-looking. Far beyond it, I saw, was the ocean, and at the edge of the coastal cliffs were some piles of rock that looked as if man might have had a hand in getting them there. I looked at the yellow Highland ox again, and gulped my coffee, and turned to Vadya, grinning.

"Well, all I can say is that if it gives milk, somebody else can have the job of—"

I stopped. Her expression was very odd, and suddenly I remembered something. *A very old castle, crumbling into the sea, she'd said, only a few stones left at the edge of the cliff... the ancient home of the Clan McRue.* We'd found Brossach, and I didn't for a moment think we'd stumbled on it by accident. She'd been instructed to bring me here, somehow, if I should escape the picayune trap on the Kinnochrue road, as I'd been expected to do. But there had been more to her instructions, I knew. I glanced at the plastic cup in my hand, and at the husky girl in the black leather jacket, waiting. I remembered that she'd always been a fast girl with a Mickey.

I'd already drunk plenty. I knew I had only a few seconds left. Whether I would then die, or merely be unconscious for an interval, depended on the arrangement she'd made with Madame Ling—the real arrangement, not the one she'd told me about. This didn't really shock me. I'd expected a double-cross somewhere along the line. It was the way she'd gone about the betrayal that took my breath away. Because she'd left me no choice, absolutely no choice at all.

I mean, the standing orders are quite explicit on the subject of several standard situations. There is the one where you're holding a man at gunpoint, for instance, and some misguided moron who's seen too many movies and wants to help his friend comes up behind you and sticks a pistol in your back. The standard, mandatory response is very simple: you instantly shoot the guy in front of you dead—the guy your gun is already aimed at, who else? It is presumed that you wouldn't be pointing a firearm at him if you weren't prepared to kill him; and you can do it without losing more than a small fraction of a second before you pivot and take care of the guy behind you by one of several prescribed methods.

Similarly, if you realize you've been drugged, you are required to get the person who fed you the dope before you pass out, if it is at all feasible—meaning if the guy's foolish enough to stick around and watch the show. The theory here is that people who go to the trouble to feed poison or knock-out drops to agents like us are obviously up to no good. They should be stopped and the practice should be discouraged.

As I say, I had no choice. I couldn't kid myself this was part of the trick we were supposed to be playing on Madame Ling. If Vadya had still been on my team, she'd have told me where we were going; she'd also have told me what was in the cup when she handed it to me.

She could probably have talked me into drinking it,

ostensibly to make our act look good, if she'd wanted to take the trouble, but she'd preferred to do it this way, avoiding the risk of argument. She'd felt that it was surer and safer, and I thought I knew why. She was counting on the fact that I'd once let her go when I probably shouldn't have, and that we'd just spent a night together. Just as I'd counted on Basil's weakness, she was counting on mine: on that well-known sentimentality I'd been known to display where women were concerned.

It was too bad. I wanted to tell her that it was too bad, and that she shouldn't have done it, but I didn't have that much time. I felt the stuff she'd given me starting to take hold, and I drew the .38 and fired and saw her go to her knees, with a look of shock and surprise on her face. I didn't shoot again. I knew it had been a pretty good shot—not perfect, but pretty good—and things were starting to blur out, and I don't believe in just blasting holes in the landscape at random…

18

"Tell them to find the woman," an oddly accented, liquid-sounding female voice was saying, somewhere outside the circle of darkness in which I seemed to lie. "Tell them to find her quickly. A shot was heard and there is blood on the ground, see? She did not take the car. She cannot be far away." A deep male voice asked a question I didn't catch. The smooth female voice replied: "No, if she has been foolish enough to get herself shot, no bargains apply now, even if I had intended to be bound by them, which I hadn't. Just get rid of her." Another question was asked, and the female voice said impatiently: "No, no, this one we will take inside for the scientists—we need all the data we can get—but a wounded one is of no value to them. Tell the men to take her down to the boat and dispose of her at sea, as usual. Tell them to make quite sure she does not come to the surface. We want no questions from our great friends and allies, the Russians. Then have them hide the boat again and wait. The ship should arrive shortly before low tide. We must get the cages on board immediately. Where is that Basil? What has delayed him now?"

There was an interval while that Basil was being located. I was aware that I was lying in the sun, probably in the spot where I'd fallen, and that a rock was gouging my thigh and an insect crawling up my neck, but everything seemed very pleasant and peaceful. I wasn't really playing possum. I had no urge whatever to open my eyes. I was happy just to lie there and listen.

"Where have you been?" the feminine voice said abruptly, quite close.

A man's voice replied, higher in pitch than the one I'd heard previously: "I have been carrying out orders, Madame. The British agent who was tailing them has been, er, removed. His car has been hidden where it will not be found."

This was a voice I recognized. I had heard it once before, in a London office belonging to a man who was dead—two men who were dead, to be exact.

"You did not let him frighten you?" Madame Ling asked. "You are only afraid of tall Americans in little red automobiles?"

Basil said sullenly, "I fail to see what I could have achieved by letting myself be killed in a collision with a crazy man. And I suggest we all get off this open heath before that British colonel realizes that he has lost contact not only with you but with the American, and starts an open search, perhaps with an airplane or helicopter. There is no real cover here, and I presume we still do not want to call attention to this place, even if we are leaving soon."

"There seems to be cover enough for a wounded girl to conceal herself effectively."

"The men will find her, Madame."

"See that they do. And take the red car away and hide it well. And then I think you had better drive up the coast with the mobile transmitter and signal the ship again. It must come with the next tide. Use the imperative code. I do not dare make any further transmission from here. They may have electronic equipment near enough by now to give them a bearing. They are getting very close. We have not much time left, due to the stupidity of those who permitted letters to be posted and prisoners to escape."

"Madame, I—"

She cut him short, apparently with a gesture. "Well, the place has served, although with more time we might have achieved better results." Something nudged me delicately in the side, apparently a toe. "Now, this one. Can you make him capable of walking, or must we carry him?"

"If the woman used the customary drug, I believe I have something that will counteract it."

"Well, give it to him." Madame Ling waited, and spoke again, impatiently: "Well, what is it?"

"What did she want, Madame?" Basil's voice was urgent. "The female Soviet agent? What kind of a bargain did you make with her?"

"Is it important?" Madame Ling sounded bored. "I certainly did not intend to keep it."

"No, of course not."

In a detached way, I was aware that my sleeve was being shoved up to bare my arm; distantly, I felt the sting of the needle. Then a foot hit me in the side, a hard kick this time.

"Get up, you," said Basil's voice. "Don't try to be clever. I know you can hear me. Get up."

I rolled over, and discovered that my hands were tied behind me. Well, I guess I'd been vaguely aware of it, but it hadn't seemed important until now. After a couple of tries, I managed to reach my feet nevertheless. Nobody offered to help me. I stood there, swaying.

Things were a little uncertain still, but they were coming back into focus. The first thing I saw was a stocky, dark-faced man watching me. I recognized him. He was the man who'd been in the back seat of the Mercedes yesterday with Madame Ling. He was also, I gathered, the man of the deep voice to whom she'd been talking in English. Except for that, I had no clue to his nationality, and it didn't mean much. English is used for communication, these days, by a lot of people who can't understand each other's languages.

Then there was Madame Ling herself. She was in slim gray pants and a pair of those cutie-boots that have taken the fashionable world by storm, but she still wore the rich fur coat. I wondered if there was something significant in the fact that practically every she-agent I met from the workers' paradise, eastern or western division, could hardly wait for an excuse to wrap herself in mink just like a dirty female capitalist.

Madame Ling regarded me in an expressionless way. I had no idea what she was thinking and I knew I'd never know. I'm as tolerant as the next guy, I hope, but I don't go as far as the shiny-eyed idealists who try to tell us that there's no such thing as race and that human beings are exactly the same everywhere. This little fragile-looking, slant-eyed woman with her smooth warm skin and heavy black hair was a product of genes and chromosomes—and of tradition and training also—so different from mine that she scared hell out of me.

Right now I didn't know if she was looking at me as an enemy, as a specimen, or as a man. She could have been thinking about something completely dissociated from the subject of Matthew Helm, or she could have been thinking that she'd like to try this peculiar Western creature in bed, just for kicks, before slitting its throat and having it tossed into the ocean. I didn't know. She gave me no clue. She just turned away and started toward the cliff-edge ruins, accompanied by the dark-faced man.

Basil gave me a shove from behind, reminding me of his presence. I looked at him at last. He hadn't changed his appearance much since I'd seen him in London masquerading as Ernest Walling, except that he'd apparently got bounced around a bit when the Austin-Cooper went off the road: he had a black eye and a cut lip. I didn't grin, but he must have guessed I felt like it, and he pushed at me again.

"Move on, Helm. Don't try any of your tricks. These

men would just love to shoot you. Human life means very little to them."

I looked at the two men he indicated. They were short, stocky men dressed in rough work clothes, like Scottish farmers or fishermen, so that at a distance they would have attracted no attention in this part of the world, except for the arms they carried—stubby machine pistols of the standard PPSh41 Russian pattern, the burp gun, that's been copied by a lot of Communist countries. The weapons were cheap and crude, no jewels of the gunsmith's art, but they were, I knew, reliable and effective. Well, as effective as any of those squirt guns can be. I still have the old-fashioned notion that there's something sloppy about killing a man with seventeen bullets when one will do the job.

The ugly weapons looked shockingly out of place against the sunny Scottish coastal landscape, just as the Oriental faces looked strange under the soft cloth caps. One of the men motioned imperatively with the barrel of his piece, and I turned and moved along after Madame Ling and her companion, but not fast enough to suit the man behind me. He shoved his gun barrel into my back to hurry me along. Off balance, I stepped into some kind of a hole and fell, wrenching my knee. Madame Ling looked back and called out an order, and the men yanked me to my feet and marched me, limping, up to where she had stopped to wait.

"You must be careful where you step, Mr. Helm," she said in her precise, liquid English. "This bluff is riddled with holes and caverns. One day it will all slide into the sea, as parts of it have done already. Once, I am told, that castle stood several hundred meters back from the edge of the cliff; now half of it is gone."

A shout from inland, where three men were systematically combing the heather for Vadya, made her look quickly in that direction. I wasn't in quite so much of a hurry. I figured they'd caught the girl, and I'd already heard the death sentence passed on her, and I didn't really want to see her again. I mean, what with one thing and another—like drugs and guns—we'd said about everything we needed to say to each other.

But it wasn't a wounded girl they'd found, but the big yellow ox. They seemed to find it impressive, even frightening, and they were covering it with their burp guns from a safe distance and, apparently, requesting permission to shoot it.

"No shooting," Madame Ling said to the man beside her. "There has been one shot here already, and the sound of machine-gun fire carries a long way. The beast is doing us no harm. Despite its barbaric appearance, it is presumably classified as domestic livestock, and some farmer may come looking for it. Let it live."

The dark man raised an arm and gave a wave-off signal, and the men, rather reluctantly, bypassed the shaggy ox and went on searching the heath. As we started on toward the castle ruins, a couple of good-sized birds flushed noisily from under our feet, probably grouse. They almost got me killed by one of the boys behind me;

I heard the metallic sound as he released his safety, and I stood quite still until I heard him put it back on again. He didn't look like the nervous type, but he was a long way from home, and I guess it put an edge on his reflexes.

Then we were picking our way over the rubble that marked the walls of the ruin. Madame Ling gestured to her man Friday, and he poked around a bit on what seemed to be an old stone floor, well carpeted with damp moss. Surprisingly, he took this carpet and rolled it up like an ordinary rug, revealing a big stone equipped with a lifting ring. This seemed to be genuinely ancient, but it swung upwards at a pull with an ease that no centuries-old hinges would have permitted. Obviously the old trapdoor had been equipped with modern hinges and counterweights.

Madame Ling spoke to the two men behind me, and then to me: "They will cover our traces, and then join the search for the girl. We try not to use this entrance often, only when it is absolutely necessary to come here and the tide is unfavorable. It was the old escape door of the keep, to be used as a last resort when the enemy had breached the walls and resistance was no longer possible. I believe the room in which we stand was originally the main hall." She moved toward the opening, drawing her coat about her. "I will go first. I will be waiting below with a pistol. There is a sentry below as well. These men will cover you from above. Please do not force us to shoot. You will live longer that way. Not much longer, of course, but a little longer."

I could see no need to comment on that, and I just watched her feel for a footing on the ladder or stairway below. She had by far the smallest foot I had ever seen on an adult human being. I looked around. The ocean to the west was empty to the horizon, blue-green and glinting in the sunlight. Inland, the rough expanse of gray rock and gray-green heather rose toward a bunch of stony hills. It wasn't exactly a lush and inviting country, but I couldn't help feeling that it beat a hole in the ground.

The dark-faced man had a gun out; another of those pocket automatics. He looked as if he might know how to use it. He gestured toward the trapdoor into which Madame Ling had disappeared. Beyond him I could see the men hunting for Vadya and the yellow ox regarding us in a thoughtful way, as if it had not yet made up its mind about us and wouldn't let its judgment be hurried. It looked, I decided, like a Texas longhorn in a fur coat and a Beatle wig. On this thought, I made my way into the hole, finding a steep stone stairway that led to a kind of chamber in the rock. Madame Ling was standing there with a little automatic in her hand. Behind her stood a man with a submachine gun, and beside her was a chubby individual in a dirty white laboratory coat.

"Here is another guinea pig for you," Madame Ling said to this man. "You can have him as soon as I have finished questioning him, Dr. McRow."

19

In a way, it was a moment of achievement. I had gone the long way around the barn with the hatchet, but I had my chicken in sight at last.

Now all I had to do was figure out how to finish the job, alone in this cave with my hands tied. It would also be nice if I could manage to get out alive afterwards, but it wasn't, I knew, considered absolutely essential to a satisfactory operation. Mac had made that clear enough.

Madame Ling motioned me away from the foot of the stairs so the dark-faced man could descend. I moved back in a docile manner. I was careful not to look too long or too hard at the plump man in the white coat. I didn't want to scare him prematurely. It was McRow, all right, a little thinner both as to hair and figure than the description I'd been given—as if they'd been working him hard—but unmistakably the man I'd been sent to find.

"On second thought," Madame Ling said, "perhaps you had better inoculate him right away, Doctor. There is no time to waste. I would like to have our statistics as complete as possible when I send in my report."

McRow said, "We should wait six hours after administering the serum. And then we can't be sure of his reaction to the culture for two days, at least not if it should be negative."

She said impatiently, "I know all that. Cut the six hours to four; give him the culture just before we embark. We will take him on board the ship with us; we will bring along all the negative ones, so you can watch them for symptoms up to the last possible moment. I have arranged for a trustworthy courier to meet us at sea, but the ship is not very fast, and it will be a few days before we reach an area where he can safely make contact. Get what you need right away, and bring it down to my quarters."

"Yes, Madame."

McRow turned quickly and hurried out of the chamber, his dirty coat flapping about his knees. The dark-faced man signaled to the men above, and the shaft of daylight was cut off as the trapdoor settled into place solidly, like the lid of a well-made coffin.

"This way, Mr. Helm," said the Chinese woman. "Be careful. These passages were not made for people your height. The McRows—McRues as they were then called—have apparently always been short men, like our scientific friend, whom you obviously recognized."

She gestured toward the opening through which McRow had vanished. I moved that way, bending over so as not to crack my skull. An electric conduit had been strung along the rocky roof of the tunnel—presumably not by the ancient McRues—with a neat glass globe every fifteen feet or so: a gasketed, damp-proof installation, I noticed. The lights gave adequate illumination, but I had to be careful not to scalp myself on them.

I said, without looking around, "Then he really is descended from the chiefs of Clan McRue?"

"Oh, yes," the woman behind me said. "That is not a fantasy, although he has many of them. There are a great many mad Scotsmen, you know. I think the damp climate must affect the brain. Certainly it would drive me to insanity if I had to endure a lifetime of it."

She was getting quite chatty. I decided that she must have a reason for trying to establish friendly relations— well, friendly for the circumstances—and that I might as well cash in on it, whatever it was.

I said, challengingly, "There's no record of an American branch of the family. I checked in a library in London."

"I know. They were all supposed to have been wiped out in a bloody feud, were they not? But apparently, when the castle was about to be overwhelmed, the young McRue sent his wife and baby to safety down these passages and went back to conceal the trapdoor and fight to the death beside his father. The wife never dared to reveal herself. She fled to America, taking the boy with her. The family name became corrupted over there as the family fortunes fell. But the story was passed on. He told it to me one night, boasting of his ancient lineage. Ancient!" Madame Ling laughed softly. "A mere two or three centuries! But his description of this place, as he had heard it, interested me, and I investigated and found that the ruins and caves actually did exist, almost unknown, and were suitable for our purposes... Just a moment. Stop, please. Open that door to your right."

I glanced at her, shrugged, and pulled the door open. It moved sluggishly, not so much because it was heavy, as because it seemed to be hooked onto a lot of machinery. There was a fine-mesh screen door beyond. The first thing I noticed was the smell. It reminded me of my childhood, when I'd raised white mice for some reason I can't recall.

Then I saw the cages, rows upon rows of them, on each side of the long, narrow room. Above them, down each side of the room, ran a long rod in bearings, geared to an electric motor at the end nearest the door. On each rod, above each vertical stack of cages, was a pulley, and from each pulley a chain ran down to the upper cage door, which in turn was linked to the one below it, and so on clear to the bottom.

That was the mechanical part of the display. The rest was just rats—or maybe I should say rodents. The cages held big rats, little rats, big mice, little mice, moles, ground squirrels, and real, honest-to-God squirrels, both gray and red, with fine bushy tails. There were other small ratty animals I couldn't identify, and I may have got some of the first ones wrong, since they didn't seem to be the American varieties with which I was familiar.

"I would not go any closer, Mr. Helm," Madame Ling said quietly. "You have not yet received your inoculation.

In theory, the disease is transmitted from rats to humans by fleas, and we have tried to make sure there are no fleas here, to simplify the matter of control. We are assuming that a rodent will eventually pick up suitable fleas wherever he may be transported. However, there have been a few unfortunate occurrences indicating that Dr. McRow's hyper-active variety of the disease manages to find other means of transmission—perhaps flies or mosquitoes, we are not sure—when there are no fleas available. So I would not open the screen door if I were you."

I hadn't the slightest intention of opening it. I looked at the collection of twittering, scratching, nose-twitching, stinking rodents. I drew a long breath, wondering if I were breathing death, and said, "They are all infected?"

"Of course." She laughed softly. "You have been wondering why I have been telling you so much, Mr. Helm. This is our secret weapon, and our insurance. If Colonel Stark should manage to locate us before we make our escape tonight, I want you to be able to confirm what I radio him about this. You have noticed the motors? There is a switch in a room below. It can be actuated either manually or electronically. If there is any threat to this place before we leave, or to the ship afterward, I will close that switch—either by hand or by remote control—and all these cages will open. They will also open automatically, after we have departed, if anyone disturbs certain warning devices hidden throughout these caves, which I will energize as I leave."

"Tricky," I said.

"Very tricky, Mr. Helm. You will note that the room narrows at the far end; it is actually only a crevice in the rock, which we have widened. The crevice goes on into the hill and meets other crevices, which come to the surface in various holes, like the one into which you fell. The switch also opens this door, allowing the animals to find other tunnels throughout the bluff. To accelerate their dispersal, a harmless gas is released that they find most unpleasant. Once they are loose, do you think anyone will ever catch them all? And if one, just one, escapes with the disease it carries, the population of Scotland is doomed. The population of Britain is doomed. And only rigorous quarantine measures will prevent the plague from spreading over the water to the Continent and further. And that is what will happen if the Colonel should act rashly. I am sure that, if the occasion arises, you will be glad to help me persuade him to be reasonable."

I said, "What if you release the plague and it spreads clear to Asia?"

"Ah, but we have a serum. It does not, as yet, give full protection—we are still checking its effectiveness, as you heard—but we are realists, Mr. Helm. We know that we can afford losses approaching forty per cent if the rest of the world suffers ninety-five to one hundred per cent. Besides, by the time the disease reaches us, we may have perfected the serum, with Dr. McRow's help."

"It's quite a threat," I said. "If you get away successfully, what demands are you going to make? I assume your country is not backing this project just to enrich Dr. McRow."

"Demands?" She seemed amused, for some reason. "Oh, yes, demands. Political demands. That is the logical next step, is it not? Blackmail. Worldwide political blackmail, such as you Americans have tried, and the Russians also, not very successfully, with your big bombs. It is an intriguing notion." She gave her soft laugh again, dismissing the subject, and murmured, "Close the door, Mr. Helm, and proceed. We call that the upper animal room. Now we pass the observation ward. I will not show it to you now, since you will see it soon enough."

I glanced at her over my shoulder, to see what she meant by this, but she was answering the salute of an armed man at the door in question, inclining her head slightly, and her expression told me nothing. I moved ahead, feeling a draft of cool air coming to greet me.

Her voice checked me. "No, turn right, please. That one is a blind corridor ending high above the sea. We go down here. Be careful, this portion is quite steep and low. Stop at the light at the bottom. The stairs you see ahead lead down to the lower animal room—where other rodents are being prepared for shipment—to the personnel quarters, the laboratory, and the cove where boats can land at low tide. As you see, we have quite an installation. Here are my quarters. Please enter."

The rest of the place, as far as I'd seen it, had been strictly business, wired for light as necessary, but with the bare rock showing, wet here and there with the usual trickles of underground water. In Madame Ling's quarters, the rock was concealed behind wallboard and wooden paneling, and there was carpeting on the floor. The furniture wasn't fancy, but it wasn't cheap, either. There was indirect lighting. There were, however, no pictures on the wall, no old Ming vases, no art objects or decorations of any kind. Obviously, while Madame Ling intended to be reasonably comfortable, she wasn't trying to set up a home away from home inside this Scottish rock.

An efficient-looking mass of electronic equipment was installed in one rear corner. Beside it, a door led into a further room, presumably her sleeping quarters, since there was no bed here. I looked for the switch she had mentioned. It wasn't hard to find, located above and behind the big wooden desk near the radio stuff—but there were two switches. One had a red handle. The other handle was black.

Madame Ling saw me looking, and said, "Yes, that is it. Black for the Black Death. Appropriate, don't you think, Mr. Helm?"

"And the red one?"

She hesitated, and shrugged. "That actuates the destruct circuit manually, Mr. Helm. Naturally we do not want your scientists poking and prying among what we leave behind. When we are through with this place, entirely through with it, we will blow it sky-high, using a remote-control device in the same circuit."

"Rats and all," I said, watching her.

"Yes, of course." She laughed quickly. "Rats and all, Mr. Helm. Now please come over here and sit down. I have a few questions to ask you."

20

It wasn't much of a question-and-answer session. At the start, at least, she asked nothing that I couldn't readily answer. I'm not a Hollywood hero, and I'm not about to get beat up just to prove how tough I am. I've never subscribed to the theory that you've got to refuse to tell a Communist something just because he—or she—asks.

If Madame Ling wanted to know what message Walling had conveyed to me through Nancy Glenmore, if I had reported this information to Washington, and if they'd had any luck with it, I saw no reason not to tell her—particularly since she'd probably already got the dope from Vadya, over the phone, the night before. She was just checking us against each other. When she got to the exact purpose of my mission here, the situation got a little tougher. I hadn't yet decided what was the best way to handle that.

"I came to find Dr. McRow," I said, stalling.

"We know that," Madame Ling said. "My question

concerned what you are supposed to do when you find him."

"Didn't Vadya tell you?"

"The Russian girl can hardly be considered a reliable source of information, Mr. Helm, either as to her own motives or as to yours…"

There was a knock at the door. The dark-faced man, stationed against it, glanced at Madame Ling. When she nodded, he turned to open. It occurred to me that he was getting on my nerves a little. I wished she would at least call him by a name, so I could have a handle to think of him by. I wished he would express an opinion on something. After all, I knew he could talk if he wanted to. I'd heard him. Well, maybe he just had nothing to say right now.

He pulled the door open, and McRow entered, carrying a couple of flasks, a jar of absorbent cotton, a pair of tweezers, and a hypodermic needle, all neatly arranged on a folded white towel on a stainless steel tray.

"You can put it on the desk, Doctor," Madame Ling said. "Go right ahead. You might explain to Mr. Helm the nature of the experimental program in which he is participating."

McRow didn't look at me. He used the tweezers to extract a wad of cotton, which he dunked in a liquid that was presumably alcohol.

"We are trying to determine the efficacy of a serum," he said, coming over to me and shoving the sleeve up my left arm with his free hand. "I'm about to inject… This man has already received an injection of some kind today, Madame," he said quickly, looking up. "There's a puncture, and slight inflammation of the surrounding tissue."

"Well, use the other arm," she said. "It was only an antidote to a drug he'd been given."

"It could affect his powers of resistance."

She shrugged. "Use him anyway. We have too little data as it is." She glanced at me. "You understand, Mr. Helm, right now you are being inoculated against the disease. In a few hours you will be infected with the culture. You will then, if our previous experience is a guide, have about sixty per cent chance of surviving."

"Sixty point five," McRow said, "according to our present figures, which however cannot be trusted beyond the first digit, since they represent a sample of only twenty-eight."

I made the calculation in my head. "That means that seventeen have lived and eleven have died so far."

Madame Ling smiled approvingly. "You are quick with figures. Of course, we are speaking only of those who were inoculated. Of our first control group of twenty—those who were infected without first receiving the serum—none have lived, but Dr. McRow estimates that, with adequate medical attention, five out of one hundred could possibly recover. These are the figures I mentioned to you earlier."

Well, people were dying all over the world, one way or another. I wasn't about to break into tears because a few more had succumbed to a cold-blooded medical experiment; but a small show of indignation seemed advisable.

"Twenty and twenty-eight is forty-eight," I said. "Where did you get all these human subjects?"

I was speaking to the woman, but it was McRow who answered, nastily: "You might say they volunteered. They were nosy-parkers who tried to interfere with my work, like you. I warned them! I warned everybody! I'm not going to spend my whole life working for pennies and having other people make millions from my discoveries!"

Under other circumstances, he would have sounded ridiculous: a peevish little boy complaining that life was unfair.

I said, "Forty-eight nosy-parkers is a lot of nosy-parkers. Are you sure Madame Ling didn't round you up a few strays on the side, people who weren't doing anything to harm you but just happened to be handy?"

He didn't say anything, but jabbed his needle into my right arm harder than seemed necessary. He knew damn well that all of his subjects hadn't been hostile agents, but he wasn't admitting it, even to himself.

His attitude gave me a hint of how to handle him, and I said, "Well, you might as well be getting used to it, I guess. After all, you're going to murder millions before you're through, aren't you?" His head came up angrily. I grinned, and went on smoothly, "Oh, hell, I'm not criticizing, man. I make my living at it myself. As a matter of fact, I came here to kill you."

I was glad I had waited until he'd got the hypo out of my arm, because he'd undoubtedly have broken it off, the way he jumped. His reaction told me I was on the right track: this wasn't a man to be tricky with, this was a man to lean on hard, just like Basil. Madame Ling and her Eastern cohorts, and the silent, dark-faced man were tough enough, but apparently they'd had to make do with some fairly mushy Western help.

McRow licked his lips. "But I… I thought you were an American agent!"

"So?"

"But surely… I mean, we don't employ *assassins*, do we?"

I laughed. "Look who's calling who names! And who's this 'we' you're talking about? Surely you don't still consider yourself an American citizen?" I grinned at him. "You, my friend, are a fool. What do you think is going to happen to you? Are you figuring on making a hundred million dollars with this lady's help, and restoring the old family plantation—well, castle—and settling down to be a wealthy Scottish laird in kilts and sporran?" His eyes wavered, and I knew I'd hit close. As Madame Ling had said, he had his fantasies. I said harshly, "Let me give you some advice, Doc, as one murderer to another. I see our taciturn friend has put the stuff he got from my pockets right there on the desk. There should be a nice little knife, about four inches in the blade. It's good and sharp. I don't see my gun anywhere, so why don't you just take that knife, Doc, and cut your throat, and save everybody a lot of trouble?"

He snapped: "Save you a lot of trouble, you mean!"

"Me," I said, "or the guys who'll come after me, if I fail. I figure there'll be about ten million of them."

"What do you mean?"

I said, "Well, I was just using your figures, Doc. You estimate your stuff will kill around ninety-five per cent, isn't that right? There are about two billion people in the world. After ninety-five per cent of them are dead, there'll still be around ten million left. And every damn one of them will be looking for Dr. Archibald McRow with a gun in his hand, or a knife, or a stone club, or nothing at all but the bare fingers and the homicidal impulse. You'll be the most unpopular man on this depopulated planet, *amigo*."

He laughed uneasily. "You're being ridiculous. Of course, unless we're forced to, we're not really going to—"

"You may not be," I said, "but she is."

I sensed, rather than saw, Madame Ling stir slightly. The nameless man at the door had also moved, as if to step forward and silence me, but she'd signaled him to lay off. She was watching McRow. He glanced at her, and looked back to me.

"You're crazy!" he cried. "Madame Ling is merely taking precautions against outside interference—"

"Sure," I said. "She's got this place rigged with more remote control gadgets than a space probe, to hear her tell it. She's going to be on the ship's radio thirty-six hours a day, after she leaves here, giving orders and ultimatums and pushing buttons like a church organist doing hot licks from Haydn. I never heard a grown woman talk so much science-fiction nonsense in my life." I glanced at Madame Ling. "Oh, don't get me wrong, Madame. I enjoyed every minute of the performance. It was real great."

She did not move. She'd thrown aside the mink

coat, and she was wearing a figured silk tunic above the narrow pants. She was smiling faintly as if she found me amusing, too amusing to stop, at least not while I was doing good work for her. After all, she'd have to break the news to him pretty soon; and this way she could study his reactions while I did the talking for her.

McRow licked his lips again. "But... but I don't understand."

I said, "Hell, sonny, there's no remote-control stuff here. There's just that black lever on the wall, which she'll pull just before she goes out the door and down to the boat which will take her out to the much-advertised ship. Since she's so insistent it's a ship, it's probably a plane or submarine, probably the latter. They've got a few, I've heard, not the latest atomic jobs, but adequate. Good enough to take her—under strict radio silence, of course—to the coast of Europe, where she'll land a load of your infected rats, and then across the Atlantic where she'll dump a big consignment on the North American continent, and maybe a small one in South America. And then home to the Orient, to manufacture serum like mad, and try to improve it with the help of one McRow, and inoculate as many of her people as possible—the politically sound people, of course; the others can go to hell—before your hopped-up Black Death works its murderous way around the world, leaving only one country in any kind of shape to take over..."

I was watching the woman's delicate, smiling face; and I saw that I was right on the beam. I saw her finger move. I didn't see the dark-faced man move—I wasn't looking that way—but I heard him. There was no point in dodging. Where could I go? I just hoped he was good at his work, and he was. The blow put me out instantly, with hardly any pain at all.

21

I woke up in a cage, like a rat. I mean, the mesh was bigger and the wire was stronger, but it was a cage just the same. I was lying on a kind of sagging chain-link shelf crimped into one side of it, about eighteen inches off the stone floor. There was no mattress, no blanket, and no other furniture except a unit of basic plumbing, quite primitive, in the back corner. The place stunk of insect spray and strong disinfectant, that was not, however, strong enough to cover up various other odors reminiscent of a public john. I seemed to be wearing a suit of crude white cotton pajamas and nothing else.

I managed to get this much information without using anything but my eyes and nose. I stirred cautiously, to give anybody hanging around plenty of warning that I intended to wake up. It seemed unlikely that surprise could gain me anything except a crack with a gun-butt, and the back of my neck was quite tender enough already.

I sat up unmolested, and found that I had the cage or cell

to myself. There were others, however, down both sides of the long, narrow hall carved out of the rock. The next cage down the line on this side was empty. There was a woman, judging by the hair, asleep in the one beyond. The hair was gray and frizzy and unfamiliar. Elsewhere, a few faces were turned my way incuriously. I knew none of them.

I decided that I was in the observation ward, the door of which Madame Ling had pointed out to me, the one with the guard. It looked pretty much like the animal room she'd shown me, except that the cages were larger, the specimens wore a certain amount of rudimentary clothing, and there were no fancy gadgets for opening the doors.

"Feeling better, old chap?"

I looked around. In the next cage toward the door— the last one that way—stood Sir Leslie Alastair Crowe-Barham, watching me through the strong wire mesh. He was wearing pajamas, too, and a pair of cheap rubber thong sandals. Looking down, I found a similar pair under my cot. I put my feet into them and stood up; rubbing my aching neck. I felt pretty groggy—not surprising, considering that I'd been rendered unconscious in two different ways within the space of an hour or two.

"I'll live," I said.

"Fortunate man," said Les. "To be so certain."

I grinned at him weakly. "Well, let's say I'll live until somebody decides otherwise. I gather they're shooting me full of their high-powered culture soon, after which it's up to Lady Luck. But, hell, sixty-forty is better odds than you often get in this racket, or so I keep trying to tell myself.

Besides, I..." I glanced around, "Is it safe to talk?"

"Oh, yes," he said. "There is nothing elaborate about this place. No microphones or closed-circuit television. They just pop their heads in now and then to see if we're behaving ourselves; and they have a full-scale inspection twice a day to check us for symptoms and drag out the positives—that is, the ones who have developed the disease."

I suppose I should have shown a friendly curiosity about the hair-raising adventures he'd undoubtedly been through since we'd parted company in London, but the fact that he was here spoke for itself. The details weren't important. He didn't seem to be particularly interested in my harrowing experiences, either.

"What happens to the so-called positives?" I asked.

"For a while, I'm told, they were kept in another ward below, but that experiment has been discontinued. Madame Ling apparently decided she didn't have the time, facilities, or personnel to follow each case to its gruesome conclusion. Now, I understand, the positives are simply disposed of at sea."

"Tidy," I said. "I suppose you've checked the locks and studied the guard routine and all that jazz."

"Certainly. There is not much else to do here. I have found no tempting weaknesses. I'm told that one man managed to escape some time ago—one of your people—but he got away from the burial squad somehow after being taken out of here as a positive. My considered opinion, old chap, is that without outside help escape from in here is not really feasible." He moved his shoulders ruefully. "Perhaps I was a little hasty in allowing myself to be captured so easily in London. I'm rather good at escaping, don't you know? It has been a specialty of mine. I had a notion that if I allowed myself to be brought into this place." He sighed. "Ah, pride."

I said, "Well, that makes two of us. I had kind of the same notion. However, I had a chance to use a little psychology on McRow while he was sticking me full of his number-one-goop. Give him a few hours to think it over, and he may be open to a proposition when he comes in to give me shot number two. Anyway, it's a hope. What's the time now?"

"I can't really tell you, old fellow. There are no timepieces in here. However, you were unconscious for over an hour. You had me quite worried."

"That long?" The various injections must have combined with the blow to keep me under longer than normal. "Well, that still gives us a while to wait. Of course, if we miss here, we may have a chance on their damn ship or submarine."

"That will be too late, I'm afraid," Les said.

I glanced at him. "You've figured it, too? I don't think there's much doubt she'll turn one batch of infected animals loose when she leaves here, but at least we may be able to keep her from distributing the rest. And this is a pretty deserted stretch of coast, and if we can get the warning out in a reasonable time, your people may still be able to seal off the area and exterminate the lousy little plague-carrying beasts before they get clear away.

There are some pretty potent and penetrating war gases nowadays. I guess they'll work on rats."

"Yes," he said quietly, "but that is not exactly what I meant, old boy. You may have noted that I am standing well away from you, and that I have not offered to shake your hand in greeting, or even as many fingers as we might get through the wire."

I looked at him for a moment. His long horse face seemed the same as usual, except for a few days' growth of beard. I drew a long breath.

"You're sure, *amigo*?"

"Quite sure. I managed to conceal the symptoms at the morning inspection, but they'll be bound to notice them when they're sorting us out this afternoon. Rather nasty-looking swellings, don't you know? So I will be no help to you on the vessel, whatever it may be. I will not be there. They are taking only negatives on board. Anything you accomplish with my help will have to be done before embarkation."

There were no helpful comments I could make. At least I couldn't think of any. I said, "Well, we'll just have to hope that I threw a big enough scare into McRow. After all, the man's searching for Utopia, not Armageddon. After thinking it over, he may well be ready for a deal."

"It's a weak reed. I wouldn't count on it too much, old chap." After a moment, Les said in a different tone: "You look pretty rocky. If you want to sleep some more, I'll watch, for whatever good it will do. Should the gates to freedom spring open miraculously, I promise to awaken you."

I hesitated, but I was still feeling half-doped and shaky; and I was going to need a very clear head when the time came, if it came. I lay down on the metal shelf again. Before I dozed off, I lay for a while listening to the stirrings and whisperings of the occupants of the other cages. I heard the slap of Crowe-Barham's rubber sandals as he paced thoughtfully back and forth along the narrow space beside his berth. Well, that was the way the virus wiggled. I might be doing a little similar pacing in a day or two, with similar thoughts for company, if I lived that long.

I woke abruptly, with Les's voice in my ear, "Time to rise, old boy."

As I sat up, I heard the sound of a key in the lock, and of voices outside the hall door, speaking a language I did not understand.

I said, "Give me a rundown, quick. What's the procedure?"

"The guard makes a preliminary inspection. You stand at the back of your cell if you don't want trouble. Then the guard backs off with his machine pistol ready and the medical gent comes in and examines one prisoner at a time, usually starting with me. However, in this case, since there is an injection to be given, he may do you first. There is never more than one cell open at any time, and the guard is quite alert... Oh, just one thing more. This medical chap of whom I spoke. It will not be Dr. McRow."

I glanced at him sharply. "But—"

"Dr. McRow is not expendable, old fellow. He is

therefore not permitted in here. Some patient might seize him and try to use him for a shield or a hostage. The work is therefore done by a young technician. The guard has orders to shoot instantly in case of trouble; to cut down the rebellious prisoner on the spot, even if it means killing the technician as well. It happened once when I first arrived. The guard did not hesitate. He used the full clip, like a man putting out a fire with a hose, regardless of what might get wet. The final score was one technician and four prisoners. No one has attempted resistance since. I mean, the way those 7.63 bullets ricocheted in here was rather unnerving, don't you know?"

"But why didn't you tell me—"

"My dear fellow, why should I spoil your happy, hopeful dreams? Shhh. On your feet, here he comes. Back in the cell. No more talking."

The door opened. There was a kind of unanimous rustle as the prisoners took up their positions. A short, broad-faced, slant-eyed man with a submachine gun stepped inside, ran his gaze down the rows of cells, and then came down the line, checking each lock carefully. When he had worked his way clear around the ward, he spoke to someone outside. A man in a white coat entered.

He was a slender Chinese youth with big hornrimmed glasses, definitely not McRow. He carried a stainless-steel tray like the one McRow had used in Madame Ling's office. He paused inside the door, looked down at something on the tray, and looked at the door of my cage, apparently checking a number. Then he came inside to set his tray on my cot. The guard backed off, holding his machine pistol ready.

"Bare your left arm, if you please," said the young technician politely, in good English.

I pulled up the loose pajama sleeve and offered him the arm. Helm, the human pincushion. He went through the cotton-and-alcohol routine. I didn't watch the final operation. If he wanted to think I simply couldn't bear to look at needles going into my flesh—after all, strong men have fainted at the sight—that was fine.

Actually, I was trying not to watch the muddy, swaying apparition that had materialized in the hall doorway behind the guard. It had a dirty chiffon scarf in its hands, twisted to form the old thuggee noose...

22

When Vadya moved, I struck. I am not a karate genius, and I can't break two-by-fours or shatter bricks with the edge of my hand—a hand good for that often isn't good for much else—but there are ways of doing it. I hit the Chinese youth with everything I had and knew, and he was dead before he started to fall. The guard came alert, looking my way, as I'd meant him to; the submachine gun steadied; and I was going to be dead, too, in another instant. Then the twisted scarf went around his neck from behind and drew up tight, and the gun clattered to the stone floor, sliding toward me.

I went for it, out the open cell door, and I was barely in time. The guard broke free and came for the weapon in a headlong dive, just as I snatched it and rose. That put him in precisely the right position for me to bring the butt down hard on his neck. I smashed it down once more to make quite sure.

It was very quiet in the ward. There was no sound

in the hall, either. I looked at my left arm, where a hypodermic was sticking out of the biceps, strangely unbroken. I noticed that the medical kid had managed to ram the plunger home before he died. Vadya had been just a little late in that respect, but you can't have everything. The odds in favor of survival, disease-wise, were still sixty-forty. It seemed likely I'd be bucking greater odds long before those came into operation. I yanked out the hypo and threw it away and went over to Vadya, who was kneeling inside the door.

I stood looking down at her for a moment. I guess I was feeling kind of embarrassed. I mean, what the hell do you say to a girl you've shot—regardless of the provocation—who comes back anyway to give you a chance for your life.

She raised her head. "I'm sorry, darling," she said. "I should have used a gun, but I was afraid of the noise. I thought I could hold him."

"Sure."

"Help me up." When I had helped her to her feet, and steadied her, she made some feminine gestures toward brushing off the dirt that was smeared on her black pants and jersey. She'd discarded the leather jacket somewhere, probably because it was too bulky. She looked as if she'd been crawling down a rabbit-burrow, and that was probably just about what she had been doing. She looked up at me with a wry smile. "I am very dirty, am I not? And… and very tired. But you are a terrible shot, Matthew."

"Yeah, lousy," I said.

"I do not think you really wanted to kill me."

I led her toward the open cell. "Let's analyze my motives later, huh? Right now you'd better lie down in here. How… how bad is it?"

She grinned at me maliciously. "Bad enough. I will probably die of it eventually, darling, slowly and painfully, screaming in agony, and you will remember it always. That you shot me, very clumsily, and that in return I saved your life."

I said, "Let's not count any premature chickens, doll. Not that I don't appreciate your contribution." I set the dead technician's little tray aside, and helped her get comfortable on the cot. "How'd you get away from all those men who were looking for you, up above?"

She gave a little laugh. "That great hairy yellow beast with the horns, remember? I decided that I could not be much worse off if he gored me or stepped on me, but he was really very friendly, although he smelled terrible. And they were afraid to come close to him. I saw you disappear into the ground with the Ling and her associate. I decided they would probably have a sentry at that entrance, but I found another way, a crack in the ground that led in the right direction. I almost stuck, several times. Ugh. I came into a room full of cages containing all the nasty little rats in the world. I was sneaking down the hall outside when I saw you carried in here. Then it was only a matter of waiting to catch the guard with his back turned. I hid in a passage across the way. It was a very long wait… Matthew."

"Yes."

"I wonder if it is that you are very clever, or just very lucky. Always you win, somehow. This time, by shooting me, you have forced me to help you escape, just as you planned in the first place."

I grinned. "I see. It wasn't just affection that sent you wiggling down a mole-hole to rescue me."

"Does that make your bourgeois conscience feel better?" She smiled up at me, and stopped smiling. "I cannot… cannot finish what I was sent here to do, darling. You must do it for me. You owe me that, now."

I said, "Sure. I'll get McRow for you."

"McRow!" She made a face. "What do I want with McRow?"

"But—"

"Oh, I am sure Dr. McRow is a terrible fellow and a menace to the world, and we probably do have people working on it—maybe some right in here—but it is not my business. Besides, you will take care of McRow anyway, won't you, darling?"

I said, "I intend to try. But—"

She smiled faintly, lying there. "I am afraid I lied to you, a little. You see, I was not sent to Britain to save the world. I was sent to perform an execution that was, shall we say, a little overdue."

"Basil?" I said.

"That is right, Matthew. Basil. I was going to trade you for him; that was my agreement with the Ling. I would deliver you to her, and she would deliver Basil to me."

"From what I've heard, she was going to double-cross

you on the payoff," I said. "You might have expected that."

"Why? When she is finished here, she will have no more use for him, and he is not a man one keeps around for pleasure. I thought there was a reasonable chance the bitch might keep her word. But now you will get him for me, won't you?"

I hesitated. "I can't promise—"

"I would not believe your promise. What are promises to people like us? But you will get him for me without promises, to soothe your bourgeois conscience when it feels badly about the girl you shot."

"Yeah," I said sourly, "the girl who fed me a Mickey so she could throw my unconscious body to the wolves. The girl who thought she was so damn irresistible I couldn't bear to hurt her."

Vadya laughed softly. "I would know better, next time, if there was to be a next time, would I not? You had better go now. Here is your gun; I took it. It has four chambers still loaded. Goodbye, Matthew."

I couldn't think of a farewell phrase that wouldn't sound sloppy, so I just took my revolver from her hand, got up, fetched the keys from the dead guard, and unlocked Crowe-Barham's cell. I looked down at the Russian-type weapon under my aim: the PPSh41, which stands for, approximately, Pistolet Pulemet Shpagin Type 41, Shpagin being the guy who designed the ugly little beast.

I said, "You know this Shpagin monstrosity, *amigo*?"

"I know it," Les said.

"Well, I'm not much good with these squirters. You

take it, I'll use my old S. and W. Come, let's go… What is it?"

Les was frowning. "But aren't you going to turn them loose?"

He gestured toward the cages, or maybe toward the waiting people in them. I regarded him grimly, remembering that he'd always been handicapped, for this profession, by a lot of childish attitudes. I'd hoped he'd outgrown them, but apparently not.

I said, "Be your age. We've got work to do; we don't want the place all stirred up by hordes of… oh, hell." I stepped back and dropped the keys on Vadya's chest. "She'll turn them loose in a little while, when she gets her strength back."

I winked at Vadya, and she winked back at me, and I knew we were in no danger of being embarrassed by prisoners released prematurely. I mean, what the hell, we were supposed to be secret agents, God help us, not the International Red Cross.

Les was at the hall door with the burp gun poised. He gave me a nod to let me know the coast was clear, and stepped out into the passage. I followed. We headed down the slanting corridor, and stopped abruptly, as Les signaled me back against the wall. Somebody was coming out of Madame Ling's office, at the lighted landing below. Les poked me with his elbow. I leaned out far enough to see the man stop under the light: Basil.

He was carrying something that looked like a thin gray metal file box. I raised my revolver and lowered it again.

A shot now would alert the place. Promises to the dying were all very well, but the interests of the living came first—and technically speaking I had made no promises. Basil tucked the box under his arm and disappeared down the stairs that led to, among other things, the cove where a boat could be landed at low tide, or so I'd been told.

After he had gone, we moved cautiously down to the landing. Voices, and the sounds of bustling activity, reached us from the foot of the stairs. I sneaked forward far enough to look down. Cages and cages of rats were being carried from somewhere inside the rock toward the water's edge. I slipped back to join Les.

"Did you happen to learn where McRow normally hangs out?" I whispered.

"His laboratory and quarters are supposed to be down there somewhere. The caves just above high-water level are supposed to be quite extensive. But the only way into them leads past the landing area, which seems to be fairly well occupied at the moment. I say, old chap."

"Yes?"

"Which of us gets him?"

I glanced at the man beside me. "After I'm through with him, you're welcome to him."

"Unfortunately, my orders are to take him alive, if possible."

I grinned. "Maybe I should have left you locked in that cell. My orders happen to read otherwise."

He laughed. "Under the circumstances, I can probably convince the establishment that abduction was not possible. One more question, if you don't mind."

"Yes?"

"Did you really shoot her, old fellow? The lady upstairs?"

"Yeah, I shot her," I said. "I'm known far and wide as the lady-killer from New Mexico... What's that?"

The sound of a cry had leaked through the heavy door of Madame Ling's office. I put my ear to the panels and heard, of all things, McRow's pleading voice inside. Caruso in his finest moment had never sounded better, to my prejudiced ear.

"No, no, I had no intention of betraying... Of course I approve of your... Yes, yes, of course I will do everything I can to help."

I looked at Les, who whispered, "What Vadya said about your luck does not seem to be exaggerated. There's our pigeon. Shall we step inside and pluck it?"

I nodded. "In case you haven't been in there, there's a pair of switches behind the desk. If anybody reaches the black switch, we'll all be knee-deep in bubonic rats. The red one just blows up the joint. I'll take the left flank, if you don't mind. I think that thing of yours ejects to the right, and I shoot better when I'm not being showered with hot empties... Cross your fingers. I hope this door's unlocked."

It was. It burst open under our combined weight, showing us Madame Ling seated at the desk, while McRow sat in the chair I'd occupied earlier in the day. He was being worked on by the dark-faced man. There was no one else in the room.

It was a fairly simple business. I mean, the conventions are quite clear on who shoots what in a situation like that, just as when two men hunt together: the one on the left takes the birds flushing left, and vice versa. The dark-faced man was going for his gun, showing a commendable turn of speed. I shot him first, since he was the more dangerous of my two birds. That gave McRow time to rise and bolt for the bedroom door, an easy straightaway mark, and I dropped him in the doorway and swung back to make sure of the dark-faced man, who was still trying to get the gun out. He might have made it and then again he might not, but I saw no reason to wait and find out.

Only then did I realize that I hadn't heard the Shpagin fire. I swung right and saw, incredibly, Madame Ling still very much alive, standing by the desk with her hand in the air. I mean, the woman should have been dead all of five seconds by now. She looked me straight in the eye, and gave her silvery laugh, and hit the black switch behind her without a backward glance, before I could get my revolver clear around. Then the burp gun went off at last.

Sudden bloodstains blossomed on the silk tunic, and the woman slid to the floor, still smiling faintly. I jumped forward, over her body, and yanked at the switch, but it was a one-throw proposition; having done its work, it no longer functioned. I thought I could hear, far above, the whirring of the motors turning the gears that turned the long metal rods that wound up the chains that opened the cage doors. There was, obviously, only one thing left to do, before the rats got out and disappeared among the tunnels and cracks that honeycombed this rock. I'm no braver than the next man, but I seemed to hear Vadya's voice in my ear, scornfully: *He did not have the courage to die in a situation that required his death.*

Perhaps I was a little braver than Basil, at that. Anyway, I grabbed the red switch and pulled hard. Nothing happened.

23

When it became quite apparent that nothing was going to happen, at least not right away, I turned from the wall to look at Les, who stood there with the muzzle of the burp gun pointed at the floor, looking sick. I looked at the gun in my own hand. There was one live cartridge left, I knew, and I had an impulse to use it. He knew what I was thinking.

"I… I just couldn't, old chap," he whispered. "I mean, she'd put her hands up, don't you know? I simply couldn't do it, in cold blood. Go ahead and shoot."

"Cold blood, hot blood!" I said. "Oh, Jesus Christ! What's temperature got to do with it?"

There was a little silence between us, during which I became aware of a faint ticking sound behind me. I went back and touched the box of the red switch. It was trembling faintly, as if alive: somewhere inside, clockwork was functioning. Well, that figured.

"I should have guessed," I said. "She wouldn't have a switch that would blow her to hell instantly. There'd be a time-delay, anything from five minutes to half an hour, enough to let her get clear once she'd pulled the handle. Enough to let the rats get well dispersed before the place went boom... You'd better go watch the hall. I'll be with you in a minute. Now you've pulled that trigger once, maybe it will come easier next time."

He looked at me without resentment, and moved dully to the door, which made me feel lousy. I mean, the thing was done; there wasn't any sense in rubbing his nose in it. I grimaced, and looked down at the slim woman on the floor, still smiling faintly in death. I went over and checked McRow. He was dead, too. At least that much had been accomplished, for what it was worth now. The dark-faced man was dead. It occurred to me that I never had learned his name or nationality, not that it really mattered. I got the gun from his shoulder holster.

The stuff on the desk caught my eye. I went over and looked for some papers of significance, secret formulas, instructions telling how to destroy the world, or save it. There was nothing that looked significant. There was still, however, a little pile of my belongings. I took time to slip my watch on my wrist and clip my folding knife to the neck of my pajama jacket. It had been given me by a woman of whom I'd been quite fond, and I didn't want to lose it if I could help it. Without pockets, I had no place to transport the rest of the stuff, so I just left it there.

As I started for the door, the Shpagin opened up with a short burst that echoed up and down the rock corridor outside. Les glanced around as I reached him.

"They're alerted, but I can hold the stairs as long as I have ammunition," he said. "Did you get that other man's gun? Give it to me."

Something had happened to him, now that he was getting to shoot at men. His load of guilt had slipped away; he looked almost happy. I gave him the extra pistol.

"Now you run along, old chap," he said. "Back the way we came. Turn right outside the observation ward. There is a passage there that leads to the cliff face, I am told. It is covered with painted papier-mâché or canvas so it won't show to seaward, but that shouldn't be much of an obstacle. Can you swim?"

"More or less," I said. "Look, I—"

"One of us must get away to give the warning. You are not going to pick this moment to turn noble, my dear fellow? After all, I already have the symptoms; I am doomed. You still have a chance, if you get away. Cheerio."

I looked down at him, crouching there. It seemed to me I was leaving a lot of doomed people behind. Again, there was nothing to say that didn't sound corny. I heard the Shpagin give another burst as I loped up the corridor. I almost fell when I stepped on something small and soft that squealed loudly; you wouldn't think there was that big a noise in that small a body. Obviously Madame Ling's black lever had done its work. The rats were loose.

I kept an eye out for the sentry from above, who was bound to have heard the racket. I saw him come into sight outside the observation ward, ducked back, waited until he was well silhouetted against the light, and dropped him with the last shot in my revolver. Below, the burp gun cut loose again.

I had a momentary thought of Vadya as I passed the ward in which I'd left her, but I knew she wouldn't expect me to stop for her and I didn't. She was in no condition for a high dive and a long swim, anyway. It would kill her just as dead as Madame Ling's high explosive. The corridor leading to the cliff was cold and dark, and I had company in it. I told myself that I couldn't catch anything from a rat that I hadn't already got from a hypodermic, but the scurryings and squeakings didn't help the morale.

Then I ran into the end of the corridor, bruising my knuckles on some kind of a wooden framework. There was canvas between the timbers. I cut at it with the knife, and daylight flooded the tunnel. Madame Ling's luck would have been in if it hadn't already run out: the sunny weather of the morning had given way to rain and fog. I thought I saw the shape of a vessel of some kind, far out at sea, but I couldn't be sure. I looked down.

It wasn't an encouraging sight. I mean, out west where I grew up, water was something you used for diluting your whiskey a little when you outgrew soft drinks and didn't feel like beer. Otherwise, except for purposes of cleanliness, I've never had much truck with the stuff. Oh, I learned to swim after a fashion in a pool liberally laced with chlorine, and I got some small-boat training along with weapons, codes, ciphers, drugs, unarmed combat, and all the rest of the stuff when I joined the outfit. But water has never been my favorite element.

I can't tell you the height of the drop, exactly. It wasn't quite as impossibly high as Madame Ling's casual mention had suggested, but then nothing she'd said had turned out to be quite the way she'd said it. It was a good two stories down, maybe three. There were sharp rocks below, on which black water broke into foam. I'd have to go well out to clear them. To the right, around a shoulder of rock, was the cove; to the left was nothing but sheer cliff, with no landing place visible, and the whole thing was due to explode any minute, anyway, if Madame Ling hadn't been bluffing about her destruct circuit. I didn't think she had been, time delay or no. All I could do was swim out to sea and wait for the place to blow and then hope I had strength enough to get back ashore somehow.

Standing there, I could hear shouts and gunshots from the cove. Suddenly there were some sharp crackling noises in there, and for a moment I thought Les must have charged the stairs and carried the fight right down to the landing area, which seemed crazy. Then a small boat poked its nose around the shoulder of rock. It came into sight, driven by a racketing outboard motor and guided by a man I recognized. Basil was making his escape at full throttle. The gray box he'd been carrying lay on the seat beside him.

I didn't have time to think about it, which was just as well. There were half a dozen small animals crawling over my feet, anyway, which made it seem a desirable place to leave. I just dove, throwing myself well out from the cliff. Suicide was not part of the plan, but for a moment, as I hung in the air, I thought I'd overdone it and would plunge headfirst right through the boat, undoubtedly breaking my neck in the process. Then Basil glanced up, startled, and threw the tiller hard over, and gravity took hold of me, and I hit well short of the craft.

The impact almost fractured my skull. The solid water was like a club. Dazed, I felt myself rushing down and down, without strength enough to make the upward turn. There were a couple of moments when I didn't even know which way the surface was. By the time I got things sorted out down there in the bitter-cold water, I was running out of air. I paddled upward weakly, burst through the surface, and something glanced heavily off my shoulder as I gasped for breath. I saw Basil standing in the boat, swinging an oar for another try at my head. Apparently his panicky swerve to escape me had stalled his motor somehow, or he'd killed it to keep from capsizing.

I let myself go under again, and saw the oar blade slice through the silvery surface, grabbed it, and pulled hard. He came right to me like a good boy. He was no trouble at all. He couldn't swim any better than I could, and I paid my debt to Vadya—and maybe to Nancy Glenmore, too—with hardly any effort. He didn't seem to be even trying. When I got him back to the boat, I saw at least part of the reason. He had only one hand to use. The other wrist was chained to the gray box.

I managed to get the body half into the boat without swamping the little craft. I swam around to the other side, heaved myself in, and pulled him aboard. I took a quick look at the metal box, recognizing it now: it was one of the standard courier cases. The weight indicated something inside besides paper: it was undoubtedly booby-trapped against tampering, with a charge that would go off if the handcuff was opened with anything but the right key, if the chain was cut, or if the box itself was attacked by a jimmy or other unauthorized instrument.

I didn't have the slightest doubt what the non-explosive contents were. Tricky to the last, Madame Ling hadn't been willing to entrust the results of her experiments wholly to the vessel in which she expected to make her getaway. In fact, she'd probably intended to use herself as a decoy if things went wrong, drawing attention from the preliminary copy of her report that she was sending to some trusted agent along the coast, using Basil as her messenger.

Like Vadya, I'd been a little surprised that she'd been unwilling to stick by her agreement and sell the man out. Certainly I'd never seen a woman less likely to be troubled by considerations of personal loyalty. But now her reasoning made sense, because Basil was the ideal courier here. A braver man, carrying a secret of this value, might have been tempted to cash in on it somehow, but not Basil. He wouldn't have had the nerve to let anyone tinker with the booby-trapped case to which he was attached no matter what the possible profit might be. Chained to a bomb, he would think of nothing but getting rid of it quickly and safely, by delivering it to the person who had the handcuff key…

In any case, I had the secret of Dr. Archibald McRow's

super-bug. I also, no doubt, had the secret of the serum that would combat it—well, sixty per cent worth.

I turned to the outboard motor and yanked at the cord. Somebody was shooting at me from the shore; I'd drifted into sight of the cove. A boat was beached there, much larger than mine, piled high with cages, but the loading process had come to a standstill now. A couple of men were wading into the water toward me, trying to close the range. I yanked at the cord again, wishing I knew more about those lousy little two-cycle motors: it's a form of machinery with which I've had hardly any experience.

A burp gun opened up, and I heard the ricochets whine past, and saw the bullet-splashes move in my direction. Then the whole world seemed to tremble, and the cliff came down.

24

The face above me said, "I am terribly sorry, sir. About your friend. He sank before we could reach him."

"My friend?" My voice seemed to come from miles away.

"The man you were trying to rescue. There's no need to blame yourself, sir. You did your best. Now just hold still, please, while I bandage this gash on your shoulder. You are lucky to be alive. Your boat was smashed to kindling… Oh, just one question, sir. Was your friend carrying explosives of some kind? I mean, there was an odd underwater disturbance a minute or so after he went down…"

By this time I was aware that I was lying on the deck of a boat or small ship. I also could remember being hurled into the water and swimming, it seemed, miles with Basil's inert body, dragged downward by that damn metal box. Apparently it had been booby-trapped as I'd guessed, and the water-pressure had sprung the sides as it sank, setting off the charge. That took care of McRow's immortal contribution to science. It also took care of my contribution toward saving the world. That was up to other people now.

I said, "Colonel Stark."

"The Colonel is in the wireless shack, sir," said the man bandaging me. "I don't know just what you told him, but he wanted to get it on the air right away. He will be back shortly."

"There was a ship or submarine or something lying offshore…"

"It has been taken care of, sir. There you are. A little rest and you'll be good as new, sir."

"Sure. Thanks."

I sat up and looked shorewards over the ship's low rail. Under the gray clouds, the shore had a different shape from what I remembered. Where there had been a headland of sorts, crowned by the remnants of Brossach Castle, there was now only a scar on the face of the cliff. I thought of Les Crowe-Barham, and of Vadya. Then I thought, for some reason, of the big Highland ox. I hoped he, at least, had escaped.

Footsteps came briskly along the deck, and I turned to see a stocky, gray-haired man in tweeds, with a fierce gray moustache. I had no doubt this was Colonel Stark, and I had a pretty good idea, having been through similar situations before, of the kind of elaborate official routine he'd put me through now. The only consolation was that I was going to have the fun of telling him that he'd have to quarantine this whole ship, himself included, until it was determined just how contagious I was…

It was two weeks before I was pronounced safe to associate with the human race again, after having so many samples taken of me that for a while it seemed likely there'd be nothing left. I was glad to see that an American doctor had been invited to participate in the experiments. Otherwise, I'd have had to rush to offer my unique plague-proof blood to my own country after the British got through analyzing it. As it was, I felt justified in getting off by myself for a day, to sort out a few uncomfortable thoughts I hadn't been able to deal with while serving as a scientific specimen.

They'd given me back the little red car, which they'd found somewhere and had tuned and filled with gas— excuse me, petrol. I thought that was pretty nice of them. I drove away from Glasgow through the usual Scottish drizzle and, after getting lost a couple of times, managed to locate a small village named Dalbright. I parked outside the churchyard and went in through the iron gate.

The rain had stopped, but the place was dripping wet. There seemed to be nobody around. The little white church was shut up tight. I walked around slowly, examining the gravestones. Every fourth one, approximately, was a Glenmore. Back in the corner stood a large memorial monument dedicated, apparently, to family members who'd once been buried elsewhere and then dug up and re-interred here by someone who felt the family spirits should spend eternity together. Here I found the gentleman of whom I'd been told, who'd been beheaded for spying for the wrong side, or for being caught at it; I also found one who'd died in a duel. I couldn't help thinking that, while we don't have many dealings nowadays with the dueling sword or pistol, or the headsman's axe, we still seem to find interesting ways of getting ourselves killed.

It gave me a guilty, regretful feeling to stand there alone. I remembered a girl who'd died in London who'd have liked very much to see this. Then I heard the gate creak, and I looked around and thought a ghost had come alive. I mean, it was a girl, and she was wearing a sweater and the blue-and-green hunting tartan: a kilt-skirt closed by a big safety pin.

I stood quite still, watching her close the gate carefully, a little awkward because of the flowers she carried. Then she turned toward me. It was not Nancy Glenmore, of course. This was another girl, not quite as pretty, but with that fresh look they have up there. She gave me a questioning glance, and went on to a new grave near the church, and began to arrange her flowers carefully before it.

I hesitated. I mean, it would not have been difficult to strike up a conversation. A question about the family would have done it. She was obviously a distant relative, or she would not have been wearing the plaid. And I was certified safe by the doctors of two countries; I was definitely not contagious, plague-wise. Nor was anybody, to the best of my knowledge, interested in shooting at me at the moment; there should be no risk from stray bullets. Still, she looked like a nice kid, and I did seem to leave a lot of dead people behind me, one way or another...

I walked quickly back out to the roadster and drove to an inn for breakfast, having passed up the ship's food that had been offered me. I bought a paper from a machine in the doorway. I had not, of course, been informed of what had happened up north after I'd left, or what measures had been taken. Security had been very tight, and I was, after all, a foreigner. Besides, Colonel Stark hadn't liked me very much. He'd made it quite clear that while, officially, he was aware that I'd made a valuable contribution by escaping alive, personally he'd have thought more of me if I'd died fighting bravely at Crowe-Barham's side. Well, he was entitled to his opinion.

Waiting for my food, I read the paper carefully. It mentioned no strange diseases. There was, however, one small item about a question being asked in the House of Commons or wherever they ask those questions, concerning the accident that had totally destroyed a secret atomic installation, previously unheard of, on the northwest coast of Scotland, near the tiny village of Kinnochrue. I closed the paper thoughtfully. Apparently they'd used a low-yield nuclear device for extermination purposes, maybe one of the tactical gizmos. It could have done the work. Maybe I could stop feeling guilty about not being able to swim well enough to keep afloat Basil's body and the burden attached to it…

Six hours later I was in London. My instructions, transmitted through international channels, were to check back into Claridge's, where the room was still being held for me. A code word slipped into the text told me that the room and phone were now safe for conversation. This meant, I figured, that our own people wanted the answers to a few questions they had not been able to ask while I was in British hands. I didn't particularly look forward to another interrogation, so it wasn't with any great eagerness that I turned the Spitfire over to the doorman, got the key from the desk, and went upstairs, limping a little. Ironically, after all the exotic things that had happened to me, the wrenched knee I'd got stepping into a hole in the ground was the only thing that still bothered me, physically speaking.

I climbed the stairs, unlocked the door, and went into the big room and started to throw my coat on the bed and stopped. There were some clothes on the bed. I picked up one item: a very simple little white shift of a dress, rather wrinkled and grimy, as if it had been worn longer than it should have been. I looked around. There were some suitcases parked beyond the bed that I recognized. I went into the bathroom and looked at the small blonde girl in the enormous tub.

"Some people knock," Winnie said. "Even husbands have been known to, not to mention people impersonating husbands. My God, it's nice to be clean again. I've been locked up in an attic for three weeks. One pitcher of water a day. You'd think they had rationing or something. Hand me that big towel, will you?"

I held it for her, as she stepped out of the tub. She wrapped it around her, and used another, smaller towel to dry her dripping hair.

"They turned you loose?" I said.

"She turned me loose," Winnie said, rubbing hard. "Do you make a habit of shooting holes in your girl friends? If so, remember I'm no friend of yours. I'm just your wife, and it's strictly a temporary arrangement, at that."

I cleared my throat and said, "What about Vadya?"

"She'll live. She sent you a message."

"Give."

"She says she bears no hard feelings for the interrogation you put her through, since you owed her something for a similar scene in the past. She says you once let a girl go whom you should probably have killed, and now she's doing the same. She says that makes the two of you even except for a bullet in the guts. She says she'll be looking forward to paying off that score, some day."

Well, that sounded like Vadya. How she'd got out of the place before it blew, in her condition, and made her way back south, I'd probably never know. How, after being in the place for hours, she'd escaped getting infected with McRow's plague, nobody'd ever know. She was a durable girl. I drew a long breath. Suddenly I felt much better, even though I was going to have to change part of my report to read failure instead of success. After all, I'd been more or less instructed to kill her.

Winnie was watching me with a wise look on her small face. "You're not in love with the bitch, I hope," she said.

"Love, schmove," I said. "Vadya and I are just good… enemies. I'd miss her if anything really happened to her."

Winnie grinned. "Well, with enemies like you've got,

you don't need friends. Now dry my back, please, and then you can order me a drink and bring me up to date. I feel like Rip Van Winkle… Damn, there's the phone. Get it, will you, Matt?"

I got it and heard Mac's voice on the line. "Eric?"

"Here."

"I expected a call from you earlier. I was informed that you'd left Glasgow this morning. Did you have a pleasant drive?"

"Yes, sir."

"You will be glad to know that the northern situation seems to be under full control. Did you, er, happen to pick up anything you didn't give the British?"

"No, sir," I said. "I had my hands on it, but it sank."

"Ah, well, perhaps it is just as well. They seem to have solved their problem without it, and we have enough fantastic weapons to worry about. Well, I will be looking forward to receiving your full report. In the meantime, the British authorities inform me that you are not a very nice man, Eric. Not really the kind of brave and forthright chap we like to work with, don't you know? Under the circumstances, I think it might be best if you were to continue your honeymoon elsewhere. I am told the Riviera is very pleasant at this time of year…"

Winnie, still wrapped in the big towel, was trying to comb the snarls out of her hair when I came back into the bathroom. I looked at her for a moment. She was an attractive girl, but the nicest thing about her, I reflected, was the fact that she was in the business from choice. She knew the score; she was supposed to be able to take care of herself. I didn't have to feel responsible for her; in fact, she'd hate me if I did.

She glanced at me over her shoulder. "Orders?"

I nodded. "It's rough, baby. A real hardship case. We've got to head for the Riviera and check into the best hotel in St. Tropez."

She turned slowly. A funny, almost shy look had come to her face. "Still as… as bridegroom and bride?" she asked.

"Sure," I said. "We haven't got much mileage out of this honeymoon cover so far, and you know him, he wouldn't waste it." I grinned at her. "Hi, Bridie," I said.

ABOUT THE AUTHOR

Donald Hamilton was the creator of secret agent Matt Helm, star of 27 novels that have sold more than 20 million copies worldwide.

Born in Sweden, he emigrated to the United States and studied at the University of Chicago. During the Second World War he served in the United States Naval Reserve, and in 1941 he married Kathleen Stick, with whom he had four children.

The first Matt Helm book, *Death of a Citizen*, was published in 1960 to great acclaim, and four of the subsequent novels were made into motion pictures. Hamilton was also the author of several outstanding stand-alone thrillers and westerns, including two novels adapted for the big screen as *The Big Country* and *The Violent Men*.

Donald Hamilton died in 2006.

ALSO AVAILABLE FROM TITAN BOOKS

The Matt Helm Series
BY DONALD HAMILTON

The long-awaited return of the United States'
toughest special agent.

TITANBOOKS.COM

ALSO AVAILABLE FROM TITAN BOOKS

PRAISE FOR HELEN MACINNES

"The queen of spy writers." *Sunday Express*

"Definitely in the top class." *Daily Mail*

"The hallmarks of a MacInnes novel of suspense are as individual and as clearly stamped as a Hitchcock thriller." *The New York Times*

"She can hang her cloak and dagger right up there with Eric Ambler and Graham Greene." *Newsweek*

"More class than most adventure writers accumulate in a lifetime." *Chicago Daily News*

"A sophisticated thriller. The story builds up to an exciting climax." *Times Literary Supplement*

"An atmosphere that is ready to explode with tension… a wonderfully readable book." *The New Yorker*

TITANBOOKS.COM

Complex 90

BY MICKEY SPILLANE & MAX ALLAN COLLINS

THE MIKE HAMMER COLD WAR THRILLER

Hammer accompanies a conservative politician to Moscow on a fact-finding mission. While there, he is arrested by the KGB on a bogus charge, and imprisoned; but he quickly escapes, creating an international incident by getting into a firefight with Russian agents.

On his stateside return, the government is none too happy with Mr. Hammer. Russia is insisting upon his return to stand charges, and various government agencies are following him. A question dogs our hero: why him? Why does Russia want him back, and why (as evidence increasingly indicates) was he singled out to accompany the senator to Russia in the first place?